Love Will Make You
Drink and Gamble,
Stay Out Late at Night

Love Will Make You Drink and Gamble, Stay Out Late at Night

Stories by

SHELLY LOWENKOPF

White Whisker Books
Los Angeles

For Toni Lopopolo

— ❧ —

ISBN: 978-0-9836329-8-6
Library of Congress Control Number: 2014933011

Editor: Christopher Meeks
Associate Editor: Carol Fuchs
Book design: Deborah Daly

PUBLISHED BY WHITE WHISKER BOOKS, LOS ANGELES, 2014

Contents

I've Got Those
King City Blues

Charlene Peck began to notice a dramatic increase in tips after she started wearing the Frilly Flirt bra from the Frederick's of Hollywood catalog during the afternoon shift at Buddy's Good Eats in King City, Monterey County, California.

Her income reached yet another plateau after an accident with the door of the salad cooler ruined her last pair of panty-hose, when she was forced to resort to a pair of conventional stockings with seams, purchased up the street, at Monroe's Dry Goods, fifteen minutes before her shift at Buddy's began.

The only other way was bare-legged, but oh, Charlene knew how much Gretchen, Buddy's wife and the daytime cashier, did not like this option. "Seeing varicose veins don't encourage customers to order the dinner specials," Gretchen said.

Charlene rejoiced in not having varicose veins, but Gretchen had a reply for that. "When you do, you'll thank me for my foresight."

Tips in general were good at Buddy's, but now Charlene was averaging twenty dollars more a shift, a fact that left her with an uneasy tug of conscience every time she cashed out.

"That's like complaining when you hit a winning lottery ticket," Wilma said. Wilma worked the station next to Charlene.

Under the pretext of filling the salt and pepper shakers and arranging the Sweet 'n Low and sugar packets for the individual setting baskets, the two were taking gulps of iced tea from glasses hidden in a bus tray. "I don't know," Charlene said. "It's like having a power and abusing it."

Wilma, who was in her sixties, huffed. "Never held the power, myself. Wouldn't still be here if I did."

Charlene felt like a barcode scan under Wilma's appraisal. "How old," Wilma said, "are you?"

"Forty-one, and so far I've made a mess of things." She couldn't help thinking about Lyle, who'd started hanging around again, insisting he couldn't get her out of his mind. But self-examination could take her in other directions, as she well knew.

"Never mind that now." Wilma surveyed Charlene with critical thoroughness. "You've got good bones and you've only just begun to sag. You've got four—five years left."

Charlene examined her chin, measuring it against Wilma's. "Waitressing's all I know."

"I'm not talking waitressing. I'm talking about power over men. You'll have to start dressing different, otherwise it looks gamey. No sheer blouses, even on hot days. Sensible shoes, no matter how funny they look. You get you a line of patter. When you kid them about how many times a night, you won't be talking sex, you'll be talking peeing."

"That sounds grim."

"Grim is when they don't leave tips for the service, they leave tips out of sympathy."

Gretchen appeared as Charlene mopped at a surge of iced tea on her upper lip. "Hate to break up the Joy Luck club here, but the Salinas Valley Edison boys want more coffee, table six wants a check, and seat thirteen wants the peach cobbler. Also, Charlene, you got to tell that ex of yours, he wants to hang around here mooning over you, he's got to order something besides coffee, you hear? And damned if you don't set some kind of record today. Both your seams are crooked."

It was the garter belt, no question about it. The seams had

been perfectly straight when she'd started out. Maybe this was some cosmic warning. Lyle wasn't the only problem. Men customers, especially at the counter, were beginning to linger, although sometimes they stayed on at the tables, too, like the linemen and installers from Salinas Valley Edison, watching her, hungrily it seemed, until the tension of it became tangible, like a sudden tule fog on the highway. The extra tips were nice—she'd even begun a modest certificate of deposit at Salinas Savings— but nice as it was, she still had to feel right about herself.

Noting with relief that Lyle was gone, she made for the small pantry aisle off the counter, where she spooned a generous serving of peach cobbler for seat thirteen, compensation for his having to ask Gretchen. Then, setting the serving down for a moment, she hitched at the garter belt, using the reflection from the glass door of the pie pantry as an aid to lining up the offending seams. Satisfied with the results, she became aware, thanks to the optical cooperation of the mirror behind the counter and the glass door of the pie pantry, the man in seat thirteen had seen the entire transaction.

A compact, almost gaunt man she estimated to be in his late forties, his hair was cut short to fend off the chaos of stampeding cowlicks. A splash of gray along the left sidewall over his ear reminded Charlene of furtive gang graffiti. Her first impulse was to ask if he'd got a good eyeful, but even as she approached him, her cheeks beginning to burn, she knew his watching her had not been out of clandestine invasion but rather of appreciation underscored by need. "Peach cobbler," she said.

"You remind me of someone I knew as a young man," he told her, his own cheeks beginning to flush, a fact that pleased her. "In some ways, I've measured every woman I've known since against her."

"More coffee?"

When he nodded, she caught him looking to see if she wore a wedding ring.

Charlene felt the tide turn in her favor, but this time it did not disturb her. It gave her an agreeable tingle. "I get off at two-thirty."

"My name is Brian Sullivan," he said. "I'm not from around here. I'm just passing through."

"Wasn't going to ask you to marry me," she said, pouring coffee. "Just to be a few days late, getting where you're going."

"Santa Barbara," Sullivan said.

"Good a place as any to be late for. I'm Charlene. If that's too high-flown for you, you can call me Charlie." No one, not even Lyle, had called her that. Wouldn't it be nice if Brian Sullivan did?. "Here, let me top off that cobbler for you."

Before he could object, she swept the dish up and started to the pantryway. His attraction for her was strong, she could feel it—but any advantage she might have had was overcome by the sight of him, both hands laced about his coffee mug, staring moodily into it.

Wilma stepped past her and began scoring the top of a fresh lemon meringue pie prior to cutting a slab. "He looks educated."

Charlene directed a spray of Reddi-Wip over Sullivan's peach cobbler. "What of it?"

"I'll tell you what. They romanticize more—unless they've studied engineering. Engineers got no sense of romance."

"What's that supposed to mean?"

"It means you maybe still got a chance to get married again—if you play your cards. Stay away from those Salinas Valley Edison types. They aren't going to marry no one. Even if they did, it's all beer bellies, pickup trucks, and Monday night football."

Charlene was considering Wilma's vision of life and its prospects in King City when she arrived at Sullivan's seat, station number thirteen. Any invasion he may have made on her privacy earlier, when he watched her hitch her garter belt, was more than offset by the quick start he made when she set the peach cobbler before him.

There was a look of hunger when his eyes met hers. The advantage was back with her again and made her smile. Her cheeks tingled as she pulled his check from her pad, set it on the counter before him. "Two-thirty," she said. "Mind you're prompt."

Charlene awoke with the gradual awareness of Sullivan tickling her stomach, by no means a disagreeable sensation, given the way he seemed to appreciate her. Opening her eyes in the dim late evening light, she began to realize the tickling was only secondary to some other intent of his.

Sullivan's index finger traced patterns she could not discern in spite of her renewed efforts. "What's that you're putting on my tummy?" There was already a fear brewing within her that he had written the words *I love you,* which, were he to utter them, sincere or not, would cost her any edge and somehow hasten Wilma's vision of beer bellies, pickup trucks, and Monday night football. She closed her eyes to seal out the thought.

"The opening," Sullivan said, "of Ravel's 'Bolero.' But don't worry, it's not the orchestral version, only a piano transcription."

"Is that what you do?" she asked. "Make piano pieces out of orchestra things?"

"That's one of the things musicians do." His tone of voice told her he was pleased with her; the nuzzle of his chin against her shoulder confirmed this. There was no mistaking his need for a shave, but under the circumstances, a scratchy shoulder was small potatoes. "There are also times when I do *this,*" he said, proceeding to make furious scribbles on her tummy.

"What—what's that?"

"That," Brian Sullivan whispered into her ear, "is *The Trout,* Franz Schubert's *Trout Quintet.* For any number of reasons, I would rather do it than Ravel's 'Bolero'."

Charlene felt herself seized by an involuntary shiver. "Is it," she asked, "something you could do around here?"

He seemed to consider. "Probably. But not for long. That's just the way it seems to go with what I do. They even get tired of it in San Francisco after a time. Besides, I really do have to go to Santa Barbara."

She drew closer to him. He definitely needed a shave, but there was a comfort to lying next to him. "I'm afraid you won't come back."

"Me, too." He spoke in a way that was not at all unkind. "But the reason I'm going there has nothing to do with an obligation to another woman." When she did not respond to this, he said, "I'm also afraid I'd drive you bonkers in no time at all."

"I don't mind a man who snores. That's very human."

He reached for her hand, squeezed it. "Snoring's the least of it."

Charlene sat up, withdrew her hand from his, circled her knees with her arms. "Doesn't anything last, Brian Sullivan?" Even in the growing dimness, she saw the same expression on him as when she'd caught him peering into his coffee cup.

"It hasn't so far," he said.

— ❧ —

Sullivan's presence in her bedroom added to Charlene's ongoing doubt that she had not got the decor right. Even in the darkness, effects she had labored over, browsed the Sprouse-Reitz store in search of, copied with great care from the features in old copies of *House Beautiful* at Paulette's Hair-Raising Experience Salon, or spent disproportionate sums of money on at designer boutiques in Salinas, all conspired to cry out in discord. It was unsettling to want an effect, being unable to get it to suit you, then being embarrassed by the result in the presence of someone who lay next to you, arms extended, naked, vulnerable.

Propped on an elbow, she scowled for a moment at a large lamp with the theme of Cupid and Psyche, which even in the dimness now seemed a reproach to the good taste she'd thought to exercise when buying it. Closer at hand, Sullivan lay peaceful in sleep, a faint curl to his lips, mere creases along his brow where there had been puckers and wrinkles. She'd done that to him; his need for her had ironed out all the tautness in him. Wilma could take her dire warnings and shove them. Four or five years? How about eight or nine? With disciplined use of Oil of Olay, how about ten or twelve years?

She trailed a fingertip over Sullivan's hip, giggling at the thought of how late he would sleep tomorrow, maybe even past the time she had to leave for work. She would make a batch of Krusteaz biscuits before she left for work and perhaps toss a Frilly Flirt or something equally suggestive from the Fredericks' catalog where he couldn't miss seeing it. Oh, he would be a long time getting to Santa Barbara, Brian Sullivan would. Why, if she weren't careful, show a little restraint, he could possibly die right here in bed with her.

She thought about such things until she heard the distant call from out in the street. Then, she stiffened. "Sweet Jesus," she said. "He's back."

Sullivan stirred with an agreeable yawn. "Who's back?"

"Lyle," she said. "You've got to believe me. I wasn't expecting this."

A sound of singing came forth in the sultry night, plaintive and lonely, reminding her of those turbaned men in Arab countries who stand in locked balconies and cry out as though they're begging to be rescued. In spite of her annoyance, some part of her was set into resonance, reminding her of the way, hours earlier, Sullivan had moistened his finger in his wine glass and, by drawing it over the rim, had caused the glass to sing.

"It sounds like—almost like Hank Williams," Sullivan said.

"Don't tell him that. That's his one trick for karaoke nights, his impression of Hank Williams. Mean son of a bitch would be pleased."

"What is this all about?"

"This is about Lyle. My ex. I had to kick him out. He's nothing but a nuisance to me now. He'll sit in that damn van of his all night and drink beer and sing Hank Williams and Waylon Jennings."

"Why did you have to—"

"Get rid of him?"

"Get rid of him," Sullivan said.

Lyle's melancholy wail grew more insistent. "'Oh, I'm dreaming tonight of my blue eyes...'" he said.

Charlene was not impressed; her eyes were hazel, and she knew Lyle was aware of this fact. "He gets mad and starts breaking things," she said.

"And so you got frightened."

"Oh, no. Lyle never raised a hand to me, only things I like. Jealousy, you know? It's tiresome. I'd start getting used to something, a radio, a sauce pan, an ironing board, and as soon as I got it worn in to where it's the way I like? He breaks it. I had this little yellow Chevy Vega? Lyle got all bent out of shape about something, and he just totaled it. Anything I like, he goes after it."

Sullivan rose to a sitting position, listening to Lyle sing for a moment, making her want to ease him back down, gentle him to sleep. "Maybe you'd better send him a message. Call the police."

"Honey." She reached for his neck and began to knead in deliberate circles, "Honey, the police isn't such a good idea."

"Are you telling me he can harass you whenever he pleases?"

Charlene was kneading his neck and shoulders with both hands now. "If I called the police at night, this being a small town, it would be Roy or Warren or Dewey who'd get the squeal, okay? Dewey is married, but we used to go together for a while in school, and lately he's started telling me he's never known any girl who could kiss like me, and Roy's been hanging around the restaurant, and Warren—"

"I get the picture," Sullivan said.

In a strange sort of way, she believed Sullivan, knew he understood how bewildering this all was to her, especially the part about his being caught up in it too. "You would never have to worry," she said, "about me deceiving you."

Lyle's singing rose in volume. "'I'm breakin' rocks on the chain gang,'" he intoned.

Charlene felt the intensity of the power return to her, then well up within her. She returned some of it through her hands to Sullivan as she continued to knead at his neck and shoulders. "Don't mind him," she said and then, emboldened, she continued, "you're perfectly safe, honey, as long as you're with me."

Charlene watched Mr. Huntsinger saw into his chicken fried steak with dedication and abandon, the two qualities he had held forth as ideals to nearly thirty years of students at King City High School. He succeeded in separating a segment of the steak from its main body, sloshed it through a puddle of gravy, then held it forth for Charlene to inspect. "I have lately begun to suspect Buddy of breading the seats of John Deere tractors and serving them up as the Thursday special."

Although his observation was newer than his interest in dedication and abandon, it came as no surprise to Charlene; she had heard it for almost as long as she had waited tables at Buddy's, and Mr. Huntsinger had come for the Thursday special. Now she had to suffer it to get the benefit of Mr. Huntsinger's observations on yet another subject.

"What," she asked, "can you tell me about—"

"About?"

"About *The Trout Quintet.*"

"I am tempted to conclude from your unquestioned radiance" he said, working at the morsel of fried steak with some briskness, "that you are thinking of embarking on a romantic venture with a person of musical tastes. Am I right, Charlene?"

She made no pretense of fussing with the table or the setting. Mr. Huntsinger had already been poured fresh iced tea; he was one of the few customers one could linger over without incurring Gretchen's managerial wrath. "Yes, sir," Charlene said. "I am giving it serious thought."

"I wish you wouldn't call me 'sir.' We go too far back for that." He sighed. "You do, of course, remember my advice to you in matters of the heart?"

She nodded, aware that some of the Salinas Valley Edison boys had dumped their iced teas in the potted palm next to their booth and were clamoring for more service.

After Charlene's father started to complain about her mother, herself, and her sisters, saying it was difficult being the only man in the house with four women, he left a note one day advising them he'd gone to Maricopa to look for work in the oil fields, had even mailed a greasy fifty-dollar bill once in a while, but was never seen or heard from again. Mr. Huntsinger, who taught such subjects as Music Appreciation, Dramatics, Public Speaking, and Senior English, took her under his wing and, to a significant extent, helped her form some of her early attitudes about sex.

The advice of which Mr. Huntsinger spoke was the essence of simplicity. She knew that, even when he first gave it. "Somewhere in the not-too-distant future, Charlene, it will occur to you to lose your virginity. I have only two suggestions on the subject. Never give of yourself for social advantage or popularity, and do not under any circumstances let yourself be taken under the bleachers on the boys' athletic field."

Huntsinger peered at her now in a way that began to bewilder her. "Has that advice been of some value to you?"

Nodding again, Charlene saw something she had not realized before as Huntsinger smiled. "Then we are ready to address your question with the seriousness it deserves. The *Trout Quintet* represents an exalted moment in our collective experience. It belongs with the late Beethoven quartets and the *Mozart Requiem* as attempts to define the sublime nature of humanity in its search for understanding. You ask me, what kind of man is it who would like such a thing?" He paused to consider the backs of his hands. "A sensitive man, a cultured man, a man whose needs reach out beyond his own experiences." His eyes seemed to be boring into her. "By any account, a fortunate man."

Charlene understood for a certainty that Mr. Huntsinger had wanted her back then, when she was in the eleventh grade, just as she saw how the very least of what he was willing to do for her now was take her home and explain *The Trout* to her.

It was Mr. Huntsinger's custom to leave her a dollar-fifty tip. When Wilma or one of the others waited on him, he left a dollar. Today, he gave her two dollars, but instead of leaving it on the table, he slid it into the pocket of her apron as he whispered his farewells to her. While he did so he took a liberty which, had he been one of the Salinas Valley Edison boys, would have earned him a lap full of iced tea.

"What was that all about?" Wilma asked. "Lofty ideals," Charlene told her. "He said to hold out for lofty ideals and not mind too much if I got hurt. Someone would always come to comfort me."

"Why, that horny old coot," Wilma said. "I bet you could."

"I know," Charlene said. "I saw."

That night was her first night alone after Sullivan's departure. She took a long, soaking bath, then put new polish on her toenails, remembering while she did so his look of raw appreciation when he'd watched her perform the same operation.

The only record store in town to carry classical music did not have *The Trout* in stock, so she had to make computer arrangements to have it shipped from Amazon. She lay in the darkness on the side of the bed where Sullivan had slept, trying to imagine how *The Trout* would sound, and then wondering if a man who knew its notes by heart could hear the piece in his head.

After a time, Lyle arrived outside and began to sing. A few shouts of neighbor protest clattered about like Lyle's discarded beer cans. Then came the sound of at least one boom-box radio, trying to drown him out, and one official sounding voice— Dewey?—amplified by a bull horn, attempting to reason with him. "Come on, now, Lyle. You *got* to stow it, you hear?" But Lyle persisted, moaning a country Western lament that sounded like the nasal skirl of bagpipes. Charlene lay on top of the bed-clothes, listening, trying to hear *The Trout Quintet* over the restlessness of the muggy night.

Mr. Right

Beth Ann has come into the kitchen for a moment to get away from Roy and Stacy. Things are slipping beyond her grasp. She can hear Stacy through the door, affable and encouraging, growing more expansive. Roy's laughter has already progressed from convivial to raucous, which is a perfect expression of the problem: Stacy has been topping off Roy's chablis at every opportunity.

For a moment Beth Ann wonders if some occult part of Stacy is bent on ruining things with Roy. She envisions taking Stacy by the shoulders, shaking this contrariness out of her. The thought relieves her until another loud peal of laughter from Roy filters through the door. Beth Ann's resolve returns. She discards plans for serving the salad first. Bring out the roast for Roy to carve. Serve it all together. Get solid food on the table. Get Roy eating before things deteriorate any further.

The kitchen door parts like a banging shutter in a horror movie. Stacy lurches in, triumphant and flushed. "If there's no more chablis open," she says, "we can start on the red."

Even though Roy has only been here for an hour and this is the first time Stacy has met him, Beth Ann notices a preemptive intimacy in Stacy's voice. "Roy prefers red, anyway," she says, heading for the counter where a pinot noir stands open to allow time to breathe.

"Will you please tell me," Beth Ann asks, trying to sound

moderate, "will you please tell me what you are hoping to accomplish?"

"Hospitality." Stacy winks in conspiracy. "Make him feel comfortable," she whispers. "He's wonderful. He's so perfect, it's frightening. I absolutely, absolutely approve." She cranes her elegant neck to give Beth Ann a peck on the cheek.

Beth Ann maintains the whisper. "You're getting him so comfortable he's nearly drunk, and you'd better be careful yourself."

This has a noticeable effect on Stacy. "Right," she says, swatting at a stray wisp of hair. "Right you are." Then she tucks at her waist where her blouse has pooched out. "The cheese and filo dough puffs," she says. "We'll stave off the problem with appetizers."

"There aren't any appetizers," Beth Ann says.

"I saw you making them."

"But you did not see me burning them."

"Burned?" Stacy tries hard not to laugh. Beth Ann can say that much for her. "You burned them?" She makes a pucker of her face in a pointed effort not to laugh, but the situation has already put demands on her and the laughter sneaks through like marauders with darkened faces and black knit caps. "You were so nervous, you burned the cheese puffs?"

Beth Ann advances on the refrigerator where she withdraws the tray on which the salad bowl and dressing cruet have been arranged. She thrusts it at Stacy, inclines her head in the direction of the dining room.

Stacy pauses just before the kitchen door. "He's wonderful," she says.

Beth Ann would have liked another half hour on the roast, but this is no time for fine-tuning. She removes it from the oven pan and places it on the silver tree-and-well platter given to her by her parents when they sold the large house and moved to the condo in Palm Springs. The roast has taken on an obscene, pretentious look that is not diminished by the wreath of parsley Beth Ann arranges about it.

The loud laughter from inside has abated. Stacy and Roy are

19

using a conversational tone, and Beth Ann begins to sense restraint settling upon the living room. In direct proportion to this feeling of regained control, Beth Ann finds her misgivings about the roast are appeased.

Then the kitchen door opens again and Stacy is standing next to her, just in front of the gas range, her exasperation apparent. "He doesn't know," she says. "It just came to me in there. He hasn't the slightest notion. You never told him."

Beth Ann is scooping Brussels sprouts from the steamer, setting them into an art deco bowl. "He knows," she says, grating nutmeg over the sprouts.

"What did you tell him?"

"Let's get the dinner on the table, shall we?" She thrusts the bowl at Stacy.

"This will be too much for him, all at once like this. He'll be frightened off."

"He's here, isn't he?"

"But he doesn't know. He doesn't have any idea."

Beth Ann feels something flare up in the region of her solar plexus. She grips Stacy by the shoulders. "Listen to me," she says. "I want this. It will happen, Stacy. There are very few things in my life I have been this clear about."

"I've got to say something."

Beth Ann loosens her grip on Stacy's shoulders. "You can say it later. We need to get dinner on the table."

Stacy accepts this, gets as far as the door before she turns. "I have to tell you now," she says. "I want you to know how much I admire you." Bearing the bowl of Brussels sprouts aloft, she moves through the door and into the dining room, purposeful, focused, but not what you could call sober.

Beth Ann watches the area Stacy has just vacated. Now it is her turn to laugh.

— ❧ —

The dinner has settled a comfortable languor upon them. Roy is still eating, taking small, appreciative bites, while leaving his wine untouched, facts Beth Ann interprets as Things Going

Well. She has assessed his genetic qualities with the same deliberation she uses in buying linens at white sales. By all accounts a handsome man, Roy's face is long and firm, not yet victim to any edema; his curly brown hair shows no signs of thinning. Even with the amount of wine he has drunk, he was able to read the small print on the label without needing glasses.

Stacy, looking reflective, even wistful, has moved most of the white beans on her plate under a large leaf of lettuce and seems to be pushing a Brussels sprout from one side to another with concentrated purpose. Beth Ann feels a splash of numbness spreading within her, seeping into warm, protected places. Roy takes one last bit of lamb roast, swirls it in mint jelly, plops it into his mouth, and chews, projecting what seems to Beth Ann a sense of indulgent mischief. "Well," he says, "I guess the moment is at hand." He winks at Beth Ann. "I'll do it," he proclaims.

Stacy snaps upright as though she had been on the cusp of drowsing. "Just like that?"

Grinning, Roy spreads his palms. "The seduction dinner was unnecessary. I'd have done it without all this—" His hand sweeps an arc over the table, indicating the elaborate setting and the remains of the roast. "I'd have done it because I'm quite fond of you."

Stacy leans forward, triumphant. "You were right," she tells Beth Ann, who watches, fascinated as Stacy focuses her best, professional, reward-the-client smile on Roy, using the raw physical charm she knows she has, like a promissory note with an agreeable interest rate. "I really appreciate your perspective on this, Roy. I don't mind telling you, I was worried."

Beth Ann feels herself begin to tremble. She reaches for her wine glass.

"It happens to be something I care very much about," Roy says. "Where will you put it?"

Stacy points behind her, toward the hallway. "It's not a large room, but it's the farthest from street noises and the living room, and there's lots of natural light."

"No," Beth Ann says. "Just no." But neither Stacy nor Roy

seem to hear her. When Stacy stands now, Beth Ann notices how Stacy's blouse has inched up again. She approaches Roy in that impulsive way she has, then gives him an appreciative hug. "This is really wonderful," she says. "Let me bring out the coffee things while we go over the details and logistics."

"No," Beth Ann says. She has begun to rock slowly back and forth. She has tried to speak but so far only a sound like a croak has emerged. Roy and Stacy are too caught up to notice.

"I have one place where there is no margin for negotiation," Roy says. "We have to be clear on that from the beginning."

Stacy waves with magnanimity. "Visitation rights are part of the package."

"That's hardly the issue," Roy says.

Beth Ann manages to get the word out. "No," she says, her intensity embarrassing her. "No," she says again, aware they are watching her. "Don't. You're both talking about different things." She is trying to hold back tears. "You're—you're ruining it." She sees Roy and Stacy exchange a glance, then fall silent, waiting for her. "He's talking about computers," she tells Stacy.

A look of satisfaction and dedication settles on Roy, giving him a mature, assured look. A man-with-a-mission look. He nods. "It's got to be Mac."

"Pardon me?" Stacy says.

"Otherwise all bets are off and I'm not your man," Roy says. "I'll help you set it up, get you a good deal on a printer, and install any software you want, but it's got to be Mac."

Although Beth Ann has decided against a sip of her wine, she cannot take her eyes from her glass. "We want to have a baby."

Roy moans in empathy. "I know what you mean," he says. "Look at me; forty-five and I still think about it. Sometimes when I see other men with their kids I wonder, is it too late? That's hardly the best reason to get married again, is it? But I see them, and I can't help myself; I wonder." He gives a self-deprecating smile. "Maybe that's a better reason than the one I had for getting married in the first place."

"There's something I'm missing here," Stacy says.

Beth Ann reaches for Stacy's hand. "I didn't tell you this before because I didn't see how it would be important," she pauses. "Roy designs and installs computer systems for his friends. That isn't his profession. It's just something he enjoys and is good at."

Roy beams.

Still holding Stacy's hand, Beth Ann is able to meet Roy's glance. "We want to have a baby, and we want you to be the father."

The look of the dedicated amateur is gone. Unseen forces appear to be tugging at Roy's face. Beth Ann is aware of his looking from her to Stacy, at Beth Ann's hand covering Stacy's. He watches while Stacy places her free hand on top of Beth Ann's, sees the two of them comforting each other, piling on the support.

"Hoo boy," he says. "Now I get it. Hoo boy, oh boy."

Stacy is an artist's representative. She has a number of actors and directors as clients who followed her from a larger organization when she and two young show business attorneys decided to form their own smaller, more select agency. To Beth Ann, who has always worked in a hospital or laboratory setting, Stacy's world seems anarchistic, mystifying, and not completely real. It is filled with people who strike her as strange and driven, even though their goals are not always clear.

Whenever their small Santa Monica home is filled with Stacy's clients and show business friends, the rooms become charged with their glamour and energy, which seems to leave a residue in the drapes and seat covers even more stubborn than the smoke from their cigarettes.

Beth Ann has neither illusions nor false modesty about herself; a girlish vulnerability causes people to confide in her, tell her intimate things about themselves before they become aware of how shy and how bright she is.

She was not surprised when Stacy approached her in the first place. But she can't get over the thought of how Stacy has pursued their relationship with such deliberation, chosen Beth

Ann over Sue, years Stacy's senior, instead of people who seem so outgoing and so much more a part of her work. The times when Stacy presses against her, pouring out her need to have Beth Ann close to her, give Beth Ann a power that pleases her but remains one she neither understands nor knows how to channel.

Watching Stacy now as she is spelling out options and possibilities for Roy about the child, Beth Ann senses what it must be like when Stacy is closing a deal for one of her clients.

While Stacy is assuring Roy that there was never a thought of him providing any funding toward the child's support, Beth Ann takes in Stacy's elegance and businesslike demeanor. Her suit is a neat tweed in a conservative cut. She wears sensible but stylish pumps. The string of cultured pearls and matching single pearl earrings Beth Ann gave her make for a sincere appearance. The one touch Roy can't possibly know about unless it has an effect on him—Stacy's very black and very silky hose are an intimate gesture for Beth Ann, a secret shared between them.

"We want the entire process to be as basic and straightforward as possible," Stacy says, waiting for this to sink in. "Nothing artificial in any sense of the word."

Roy is taking sips of coffee. Beth Ann can see him responding to the situation and to the overall effect of Stacy, who is working him, weighing each moment, reaching out to touch him to make an emphasis. Watching Stacy, Beth Ann is dazzled. For a brief moment, she suffers a pang of loneliness, wishes Stacy were touching her, too.

"Sure," Roy says. "Of course. Everything should be—"

"Natural," Stacy says.

"Right," Roy says. "Natural."

Beth Ann is smiling now. The word is shimmering out there in front of them. "Natural," Beth Ann says.

Roy could take it in a number of ways, use it as a means of being crude about them, an excuse for backing out. But he doesn't; he is buying it. Beth Ann knows the situation has him completely enthralled. Stacy has him hypnotized.

"I mean, look at it this way," Stacy says, projecting bravado. "Beth Ann spends a lot of time in and around laboratories. When the child goes to visit her, we don't want him or her to take a look at a rack of test tubes and have a traumatic response, right?" She pokes Roy affectionately on the knee.

Beth Ann feels her stomach contract, fearing Stacy has ridden her exuberance a bit too far.

Roy nods, even manages a laugh. "Oh, sure," he says, "sure." From his affirmative emphasis, Beth Ann is positive now that he is aware of Stacy's black silk hose.

"One of the most important factors in this decision," Beth Ann explains, "is that we see it as a way, a wonderful way to affirm and solemnize our relationship."

This has the desired effect. Roy is in their grasp. Beth Ann can see it. She is excited; her eyes dart toward Stacy. It is a small moment of wonderful power between them.

"Suppose," Roy says, "suppose I really got to liking the idea?" He focuses on Stacy. "What you said before about visitation rights. It would be good for the child to have that—"

"Polarity," Beth Ann says. "Meaningful exposure to both sexes."

"Yes. Polarity."

And now Stacy works the closing argument. "Then it's all settled. We're agreed."

Beth Ann is tense at the long silence, aware of Stacy watching her, silently warning her: Let Roy make the first sound.

Roy lifts his cup, sipping at dregs.

Beth Ann thinks to replenish his coffee but feels Stacy's firm gaze, forbidding even this.

"Hoo boy," Roy says. "Fatherhood. Hoo boy, oh boy."

Stacy winks. Now Beth Ann feels free to pour more coffee.

"What the hell," Roy says. "Why not?" He sips coffee, sets the cup down, picks it up, takes another sip, sets the cup down again. "I mean, why the hell not? Let's go for it." He stands, moves awkwardly toward Stacy, recovers with a courtly bow, then draws her to her feet and begins to wheel her into an impromptu waltz for some moments, stopping now, his self-consciousness winning an arm wrestle with his excitement. "Okay, what are the mechanics?" He mistakes the response he gets from Stacy. "Not those mechanics." He laughs. "That I don't have to be told. I mean the timing. I need to know when."

For a moment Stacy's face seems stripped of its vitality. A vulnerability Beth Ann has not seen in her before appears now. When their eyes meet, Beth Ann sees a flickering of anguish and fear. She has never felt so close to Stacy, understood her so well. She reaches out to invite Stacy to her arms, comforting her even while looking past her toward Roy, showing them both how it is going to be.

The Ability

In order to follow the route Mrs. McNeely has marked for her, Rachel has to probe her way across campus to the site of the first large X drawn on the map, to the Service Center, where her picture is taken by a man young enough to be a student. His attitude makes it clear he would rather be reading his paperback copy of *Heart of Darkness*.

After he has stapled a frontal shot and a right-facing profile to Rachel's application, she sets forth in the direction of the second X, the Administration Building, a task that seems easy enough until she presents herself at Room 214, as instructed. "Mr. Famillian?"

A genial-looking, overweight man, with frameless bifocals and quite a bit of gold in his teeth, smiles at the sight of her visitor's badge. "Uh-oh," he says, and then shakes his head. "Here we go again. Look it here," he says with a note of triumph. "You've got the wrong building. I know all about you, though. You one of McNeely's people."

Rachel remembers the admonition from someone sitting next to her before her preliminary screening and testing: Sometimes after they begin to develop an interest in you, they arrange situations to see how you behave under stress. Rachel smiles at the man. "I'm looking for the Administration Building."

The man returns her smile. "You think I look like an administrator? I can see right off, you've never worked at a university before."

Rachel shakes her head. "Law office. Public relations. A couple of radio stations, but never a university. "

"That map they give you," the man says. "It is just plain wrong. Mrs. McNeely, she know it wrong. You understand what I'm saying?"

Rachel forgets her caution. "If she knew it was wrong, why did she give it to me?"

"She give it to you because once a university starts something, you need an act of God to change it. I hope my saying it that way doesn't offend you, but it's true. You get a job here, you remember Earl B. Willis the one who revealed the truth to you. The only way to get that map changed is to use the whole printing of it. "

— ❧ —

When Rachel finds the Administration Building, and Room 214 within it, she presents her folder to Mr. Famillian, as directed. Mr. Famillian frowns at his watch. "We wondered what kept you," he says before inviting her to sit. When he thumbs through Rachel's folder, the sounds he makes remind Rachel of a dog, whimpering to be let out.

"I see from this that you have the ability."

"Excuse me?"

"Mrs. McNeely, who gave you your screening interview and tests, says in her notes that you have the ability, and from what I can see here—" He holds forth a document Rachel recognizes as one of a battery of tests she took. "—She's right." He gives Rachel a solemn nod. "The test has been wrong about some things, but never about this." He returns his attention to her application. "The types of jobs you're applying for? They all reveal something about you."

Rachel tries to make eye contact. "I have good references, I keep jobs for a long time, and I've never been fired."

"I'm talking about hidden agenda." Mr. Famillian flicks at the application as though there were a bug on it. "Perhaps we should discuss why someone with your experience would apply for a job beneath her abilities."

Rachel sighs. "All right." She hopes an intake of breath will slow down the color beginning in her cheeks. "I want to finish my education. I understand full-time employees get up to twelve units of tuition remission a year."

"And you thought you could do well by your work and attend classes at the same time."

"Yes," Rachel concedes. "That's what I thought."

Mr. Famillian smiles, which Rachel interprets as his triumphant discovery of her duplicity. "Very nice, indeed." He scrawls notes on the margin of her application.

Rachel is now convinced her goal has been denied her. But then Famillian says, "And commendable, too. Of course, you can see why we'd be suspicious when a person with high verbal skills applies for a clerical job. "

"As a matter of fact," Rachel shrugs, "I can't."

"My dear Miss—" Famillian scans the application. "—Moss. You have no idea." A note of distaste insinuates into his voice, which he lowers to a more conspiratorial register. "You have no idea how many people hope to take these jobs to subsidize themselves while they work on a screenplay. The tests can't always sift the screenplay people out, you understand, so we find ourselves at an impasse. Despite all the publicity to the contrary, universities are conservative places. Once we start something or hire someone, change is not easily effected. "

"A screenplay," Rachel says, "is the farthest thing from my mind."

Famillian makes some added notes on the margin of her application. "I'm relieved to hear that. Since I'm your last real obstacle before you can be hired, I can even tell you I trust you. I don't think you *will* try to write a screenplay. But there's something else to be reckoned with. "

Rachel waits him out.

Once again Mr. Famillian flicks her application folder. "The job you've applied for is quite out of the question. Your aptitude test shows you have the ability, and so I'm very much afraid it's either that or nothing."

— ❧ —

When Rachel reads the official description of her job for the first time, she is sitting in the office of Karen Woodhouse, the person who will be her supervisor.

Everything about Karen Woodhouse's fitted suit and her office décor suggest a mannered neatness to Rachel, a Maginot Line of defense against lack of seriousness. "You don't have to be embarrassed," Karen Woodhouse assures her. "Laughter, I'm told, is a very healthy response, provided, of course, the laughter is not derisive in intent."

Rachel sees a name plate on her desk advising all who see it that Karen Woodhouse has a Ph.D. After she has been at the job for a time, Rachel will realize how much her supervisor enjoys being called Dr. Woodhouse and will discover that her degree is in religious studies. When Karen Woodhouse rises to move from behind her desk, Rachel is struck by how short the woman is and quickly resolves not to remain standing in her presence. "I'm laughing because—" Rachel looks at her job description, printed on embossed stationery watermarked with the university seal. "—because I'm not sure I can do this."

"Of course, you can do it," Karen Woodhouse delivers the affirmation with a firm nod. "Your test results give us convincing proof. But it isn't as easy as it sounds. The job requires concentration and sincerity."

Rachel tries to project solemnity by tenting her hands.

"This is often a high-pressure work environment," Woodhouse continues, "and while I am sympathetic to the idiosyncratic nature of responses to that pressure, there is something I need to impress on you before I show you your work station."

Even though Rachel is not as sure as her employers about her ability to deal with the requirements of her job as defined in the official description, the lure of being able to enroll in two courses a semester at no charge is irresistible. She manages to present a serious attitude to her supervisor as encouragement for her to continue.

"This department," Karen Woodhouse explains, "has a

dress code reflecting the serious intent of our mission. Suits or dresses, please." Rachel rises before discovering she has been premature.

— ❧ —

"Did she—" Rachel's office neighbor lowers her voice to a whispery sincerity. "—Try to impress you with the absolute need for discretion?"

When Rachel laughs at the woman's convincing imitation of Karen Woodhouse's reedy contralto voice, a bond of sorts is established between them. They are of similar age, but when Rachel compares their outward appearances, she feels a world apart, somehow restrained if not outright conservative.

The young woman has managed to observe the rigorous intent of Karen Woodhouse's dress code for her subordinates; she is wearing a suit, but it is made of denim, enhanced by a silky blouse with bright-colored blotches and dots. She wears three earrings on each lobe. Her glossy dark hair is braided in the most complex corn-row pattern Rachel has ever seen, featuring bright ceramic beads that seem to click merrily when she laughs.

"Ardella Sims," she says. "My specialties are what Woodhouse calls the dire scenarios. Condolences, urban hopelessness, anomie in minority groups, and brain drain." When Rachel raises an eyebrow at the last designation, Ardella explains. "Universities get worried when their top scholars are lured to other schools or the private sector for more money."

Nodding, Rachel introduces herself. "I'm afraid I don't have a specialty yet."

Ardella's scrutiny of her is intense, even critical, but not unkindly. "My guess for you," she says, "is thank-you notes, rediscovering the humanities, and—" She chews a thumbnail for a moment. "—And politics."

"I'm not very political," Rachel offers.

Ardella's hair beads click from her nod. "Definitely politics."

In the following weeks, Ardella's surmise proves to have been prescient. Rachel is given assignments to write letters of thanks which will be signed by assistant deans, full deans, and

31

in one notable instance a university vice-president. The thanks are for financial and other gifts to the university, for observations about university life from affluent alumni who are seen as potential benefactors, and for favorable mention of the university in periodicals.

When Rachel is not actually writing letters, she is, to use Karen Woodhouse's verb, "screening" newspapers, magazines, and newsletters that arrive daily and for which she and Ardella have responsibility. Any mention of the university is to be acknowledged with a cheery letter to the source, then filed according to a numerical system ranging from minus-five to zero, and zero to plus-five, the pluses representing potential contributors of money, goods, or services to the university, the minuses to be cultivated for future elevation to pluses.

Within two weeks, Rachel has been commended for turning a minus—a snide report of the women's tennis team, NCAA finalists for the last three years, on the cusp of disbanding for lack of funds while the men's tennis team, notable for lackluster performance and a recent steroid scandal, getting two million dollars worth of new facilities—into the plus of a donation from a sporting goods manufacturer. As well, she has ghost written such elegant thank-you notes that two donors of funds to the university general fund have increased their original gifts.

"It was all there to be seen in your test results," Karen Woodhouse says, showing Rachel the follow-through memos on her work and giving her a Friday off. "Go shopping. Play hard, then get plenty of rest. Your first real test comes Monday." She has never before winked in Rachel's presence, but now she does.

"Can you give me a hint?" Rachel asks.

Even though they are alone, Karen Woodhouse looks about as though they might be overheard. "How are you on condolence?"

"I guess I'm all right."

Karen Woodhouse shakes her head. "Guesswork is a bad business in condolence, Rachel."

"Maybe you'd better give it to Ardella."

The disapproval continues. "I'm afraid not," she says.

Rachel has seen some of Ardella's letters and memos. "But why? She's good. I mean, very good."

"At one time there was no question about Ardella's suitability to this assignment, but you see there is a down side."

"How can a job like this have a down side?"

Karen Woodhouse closes her eyes for a moment, then she lowers her voice to a whisper.

— ❧ —

Later, Ardella stands at the side of Rachel's desk, deftly keeping a wadded-up Coca-Cola cup in the air, using only her feet, knees, and legs to maintain it, a considerable accomplishment with her spike heels. "She really said that?" Ardella asks.

Rachel nods.

"I didn't give her that much credit." Showing off with a kick from the back of her shoe, Ardella almost loses her balance. "What were her exact—" she lunges again, catches the wadded cup on her knee, sends it in a high arc, "—her exact words?"

"She said you were entering a burn-out curve."

"Shoot." Ardella lets the cup fall. "I'm not burning out, I'm just getting cynical. You will, too."

— ❧ —

Karen Woodhouse answers her private-line telephone, listens, then waits for a respectful moment. "Yes," she says. "We're on our way."

Rachel begins to stand, then sinks back into her chair when she realizes Karen Woodhouse has more to say.

"I want to remind you of a personal tendency of yours," Woodhouse begins. "An idiosyncrasy, really." She waits for a nod from Rachel before she continues. "We are going to the Office of the University President. This matter is about grief. Condolence. And—"

"And?" Rachel says at length.

"You have a tendency to laugh under stress. Please consider

the possibility for laughter under such circumstances being misconstrued."

— 🌢 —

With the possible exception of a sweeping view of the campus from its fourth-story perch, the most notable feature of the university president's office is its almost complete lack of books.

A vision of Ardella comes to Rachel, and she has to tighten her jaw to keep from smiling, an effort she is forced to enhance when she notices a Nordic Track exercise unit off in one corner.

Rachel and Karen Woodhouse are seated next to one another on a large sofa, its buttery leather expanses quite comfortable for Rachel but threatening to swallow up her superior.

Facing them, perched on the edge of the university president's desk, is a man of middle age. Trim, with blow-dried gray hair, his Phi Beta Kappa key prominent against his dark vest, he describes himself as the president's liaison. "Call me Chuck." The university president is not in the room with them, but Chuck hitches his head to the unoccupied chair behind the desk as though he were. "Fred—Dr. Werneke—needs some special handling on this one." He flashes a conspiratorial smile at Rachel. "Very special."

From the corner of her eye, Rachel can see Karen Woodhouse nodding in a solemn tempo.

— 🌢 —

Ardella Sims hoots. "Did you laugh when Chuck told you what it was?"

Rachel is trying to concentrate on the screen of her computer. A few moments earlier, she'd been focused on a sheet of blank paper in the printer she shares with Ardella. Before that, she was crossing out sentences she'd written on a legal-size pad.

"You did, didn't you?"

Rachel sighs. "But not at what he said."

"You laughed at Woodhouse," Ardella persists. "You laughed because she was so damned serious."

34

Rachel spins around in her chair. "I don't see how you can do this stuff. I don't see how anyone can do it."

Today Ardella is wearing elaborate lace-up boots which she now props on the edge of her desk. "You," she says. "You can do it. Seems to me you have done it."

Rachel bites at her lip. "But I don't see how."

For a long moment Ardella appears to conduct an internal argument. At length, she sighs in what appears to Rachel as resignation from having a sworn secret pried loose from her. "Okay. This man Taft I used to fool around with? He's an actor. I watched him rehearse a play where he had a crying scene. The director made him do that scene three, maybe four times in a row." Ardella's hair beads crackle as she shakes her head. "What man you know can cry four times in less than an hour?"

"What does this have to do with the dumb condolence letter I'm supposed to write?" Rachel returns to her note pad, looking at beginnings she has already crossed out, trapped in her frustration.

"I'm giving you the store is what it has to do with the dumb condolence letter," Ardella says. "I'm giving you the way it's done by other professionals." She springs to her feet, moves to Rachel's desk and spins Rachel around to face her. When she is sure she has Rachel's attention, Ardella turns her palms upward and smiles. "When Taft was a boy, both his parents had to work to make ends meet."

"Ardella!"

"Well, if you'll listen, you'll get the connection. Taft was raised by his grandma, so he came to love her dearly, and when she died—"

I can't take this anymore." Rachel slams her note pad on the desk, and leaves the office. In the anteroom, she nearly bowls over Dr. Woodhouse, a fact that does nothing to ease her temper.

"Is everything—all right?" Karen Woodhouse appears solicitous.

"You mean, am I cracking under the pressure?" Rachel surprises herself by snapping.

"I heard voices." Karen Woodhouse inclines her head toward the office Rachel shares with Ardella Sims. She seems to appreciate the potential for double entendre in her response, but not before a bitter laugh escapes from Rachel.

"You don't think any of this is strange?" Rachel challenges her.

"Grief is a very complex thing." Karen Woodhouse places a hand of consolation on Rachel's arm.

Rachel retreats a step. "I'll tell you what a complex thing is," she says. "A complex thing is when the president of a university needs a ghost writer to produce a condolence letter for the death of a large donor's pet cat."

"As I understand it," Karen Woodhouse whispers, "Binky was a very gifted animal."

Rachel cannot trust herself to respond with civility. She pivots around Karen Woodhouse and leaves the Development Procedures office, exiting the Administration Building from the rear. Crossing through the Memorial Garden for Departed Alumni, she scans the tables, looking for an empty at one of the small food concessions in the Commons Building. Even though she is attracted to Greg, the laid- back, self-deprecating teaching assistant from her political science class, she begs off on a chance to sit with him, settling down alone with a large Diet Coke.

She has worked her way through a good portion of her drink and has begun to feel better when Ardella plunks down next to her, silently offering Rachel half of her Shabazz individual-serving bean pie. When Rachel shakes her head, Ardella presses forth as though there had been no interruption in their conversation.

"The trick is," Ardella says, "whenever Taft has to portray sadness, he thinks about his beloved grandma. No matter what the sadness, Taft thinks about his grandma. You get the drift?"

Rachel sips more Diet Coke. "The only people in my family I care about," she confesses, "are still alive."

"The person doesn't have to be in your family," Ardella says. "It can be anyone." She nibbles at the bean pie. "Most of

the people in my family, I'd laugh if I thought of them dead."
She studies Rachel for a moment. "You too young for Bobby
Kennedy?"

"I don't know. I'm not sure. Do you use him?"

Ardella's hair beads click. "Don't get me wrong," she says,
"it isn't a color thing, you understand, and he was a good man,
but the feeling has to come from the deepest heart." Her face
opens in as broad a smile as Rachel has ever seen from her. "I
can't help myself, especially since I made the association."

Rachel watches in fascination as Ardella's smile continues
but her eyes begin to brim with tears. "My main man," Ardella
says, "is Jimi Hendrix. All I have to do is think of that dude, and
I lose it."

– ❧ –

I can see," Chuck tells Rachel, "that you have an empathetic nature. Very empathetic." They are sitting at a small table in
the tea house overlooking the pond just beyond the Garden of
Departed Alumni. Chuck has ordered the most expensive item,
the Pacific Rim Option, an earthenware pot of green Japanese
tea, and a large dish filled with crusty sweets, from which he
motions for Rachel to help herself.

"I felt a lump in my throat when I read the letter, and I don't
mind telling you, Fred—President Werneke—damn near cried
when he signed it."

From the moment of Chuck's invitation to tea, Rachel has
suspected him of an agenda in which every step has been calcu-
lated. She is waiting him out but giving him nothing in the
process. Even though the tea is frothy and refreshing, the pastry's stuffing is delicious, she has not acknowledged this to him
nor has she responded to his praise about what she has come to
think of as The Binky Letter.

She is aware of his close scrutiny, made to feel for a moment
like a piece of carry-on luggage being screened by airport security. For what purpose? For what hidden weapon? For the ingredients of what home-made time bomb? She scarcely has the time

to consider Chuck's motives when her attention is caught by Ardella Sims, the deep-tufted grass of the garden presenting a considerable obstacle for her high heels.

Moving with a measured sway, Ardella is carrying the distinctive bright yellow transmittal envelope of university mail. She is at close enough range for Rachel to see her offer of a broad wink. The gesture is just bold enough for Rachel to take heart from it and maintain her non-committal coating before Chuck.

"I don't see how you do it," he says, "but that's what makes the Ability so special." His hand describes an arc before the Garden of Departed Alumni. "I wish we'd had you with us when this was being set up." He shakes his head. "I still think five thousand dollars isn't enough."

Before she can stop herself, Rachel's curiosity gets the better of her. "Excuse me? Isn't enough for what?"

"I thought you were in the loop." He hitches his garden chair closer. "Well, the hell with it. I'll tell you anyway. You either trust someone—or you don't. You know, of course, how this place got its name?"

"Doesn't take much imagination," she says, angry with herself after realizing that this is the step just before the one she has been set up for. "It's enough," Chuck affirms, "but also for a discreet few—I have to emphasize that discreet few part—who, for a five-thousand-dollar donation, can have their ashes scattered for all time on the grounds of their alma mater. "

As this registers on Rachel, a chill passes through her and she touches her shoulders for comfort. Chuck pours her more tea then pushes the platter of pastries toward her. "I'd still like your input on the Memorial Garden overview, but that isn't the reason I invited you here today." In the long afternoon shadows, his eyes are flinty reflections of an emotion Rachel cannot read.

— ❧ —

The sounds of Ardella's industry are daunting to Rachel. She has been slow all morning, puttering with the journals and newspapers she routinely reads for mention of the university, or thumbing through her *Bartlett's Familiar Quotations* and the *Oxford Companion to English Verse* for inspiration toward the new project Chuck has given her. "Process" is the name Karen Woodhouse has given to this kind of fidgeting. "The Process of the Ability is fermenting within you."

"And if you aren't careful, it will spoil your dinner," Ardella responds. Over the last few weeks, there has been a notable upswing in Ardella's mood from the cynical to the chipper. In similar fashion, Ardella's footwear has seemed to change from Doc Martens and combat boots to the steeply elevated and the ethereal. Today, Ardella is even humming as she addresses her computer.

A few moments after the university mail is distributed, Karen Woodhouse enters their office without knocking, flustered and coloring. Rachel, already distracted, is the first to notice.

"I seem," Karen Woodhouse says, holding a page torn from a note pad, "to have a secret admirer."

Interested, Ardella looks up. "I didn't think you were interested in sex."

"Not all admirers are necessarily after sex." Karen Woodhouse's reproof carries a thrust of her jaw with it. After a moment, she turns away from Ardella and lowers her eyes to the paper in her hand. "But you're right," she says. "This one does seem to be. 'It's difficult to see you at such close hand,'" she reads, "'and think the attraction is all one-way. I may be reading the signals incorrectly, but I think you're interested, too. I think we both have yearnings.'"

Rachel has begun to feel uneasy. She has seen this kind of note paper in Karen Woodhouse's hand a number of times; it is standard issue in a university. But there is a ring of familiarity to the phrasing of the words.

"You both have to be honest with me," Karen Woodhouse explains. "I'm quite nearsighted. What often begins in all innocence as a vacant stare is sometimes misinterpreted by men, and

I wouldn't want anyone to think—" Her struggle appears to be exquisite. "On the other hand, if an individual with high moral values should find me—"

Rachel feels her cheeks begin to burn. "The note isn't for you. I'm almost certain it was written by the teaching assistant in a course I'm taking. He signs his notes with a very elaborate capital G."

Karen Woodhouse scans the note then thrusts it at Rachel. "The communications coming into and going out of this department are highly sensitive and I should think you had enough experience with us by now to know you must keep your personal life as a thing apart." She moves from the room without looking at either of them.

Aware of Ardella watching her, Rachel turns to her desk, picks up her *Oxford Companion*, then begins looking for clues to get her connected with Chuck's assignment.

Ardella allows her some time to riffle through pages. "Hey, girl," she says. "You got yearnings?"

Rachel considers this for a moment, then nods. "Yeah," she says, "I guess I do."

"Well, congratulations, friend." Ardella is at Rachel's side, first for a high five, then for a hug. Although they have shared the office and confidences for nearly a year, this is the first moment Rachel senses they have indeed become friends.

Rachel likes the virtual anonymity of her one-room apartment in a converted garage . Because the apartment was built without permit or zoning variance, the owner has made no effort to make the entryway or even the street address obvious. With the exception of the mail delivery, hardly anyone knows there is a 1460-A on Olive Street.

Rachel is surprised when, quite early one Saturday morning, she hears a banging at the door. Recalling occasional intrigues with a marauding raccoon, she turns on the porch light, thinking to frighten away her intruder, but then, thinking it might be

Greg, irritation conflicts with tenderness. She already knows of the imbalance: He cares for her more than she cares for him. He has taken to telephoning, trying not to sound desperate.

Turning on the porch light serves to inspire more banging and now a voice Rachel recognizes. When she opens the door, Ardella clicks past her, plops herself down into the stuffed chair near the bed, and removes her point-toed pumps. "Got anything to drink?"

"Some wine I use for cooking."

"I mean soothing stuff, things women give their friends who have troubles. "

"If you have cramps, I can give you some aspirin."

"Not that kind of troubles," Ardella snaps. "Things like chamomile tea, or rose hips. Things for men trouble. "

"I have some regular tea," Rachel offers. "Lipton's, I think."

Ardella eyes her skeptically. "You think regular will do it?" Rachel moves to the tiny Pullman kitchen and draws water into a kettle. "I don't know what the problem is. "

"I've been dumped is what the problem is. The son of a bitch is getting married, and it isn't going to be to me."

"Who? What are you talking about?"

Ardella massages her ankles and feet. "Don't tell me you didn't know. I know you're naive, but you must have seen it."

Rachel shakes her head.

"Shoot," Ardella says with some passion. "You were in it." Rachel forgets all about the tea until the kettle begins to whistle. She puts too many tea bags in the pot, pours the water, and reaches for cups. "I don't understand."

Ardella accepts her tea, cools it with a few breaths, sips, and then laughs with bitterness. "You were doing some special work for Chuck?"

"For Dr. Werneke. For the history department, really."

"But you turned it in to Chuck, right?"

"He looks at everything I do now."

Ardella hoots. "I'll bet he does." She gives a critical look at the tea, takes a large sip, and then seems to be waiting for some effect. "You were writing some highly personal letters to a woman historian who had a lot of qualifications. Among them, I believe, were a lively, inquiring mind, a sense of human drama, and a special, hybrid vigor." While Ardella speaks, Rachel has set her own tea down and has grabbed Ardella by the shoulders. "Where did you hear that?" She begins to shake Ardella. "How could you know such things?"

Ardella waits out the shaking spell until Rachel stops of her own embarrassment. "Because there was no historian. The letters you wrote for him, he was using on me—and I've got to tell you, Sweetie, they worked."

"That day I was with him at the tea house and you came by?" Rachel asks, the weight of it hitting her. "You weren't winking at me."

"I was having some fun, putting the tease on him. You know, make him suffer a little?" She utters a rueful laugh. "He was already suffering so badly, he wanted to make sure, so brought in you."

"You actually fell for him. Because of what I wrote."

Ardella's eyes water. "He was cool about the racial difference. I thought he'd be the same way about the gap in our ages."

"How horrible," Rachel says. "How very horrible. Things I believed, things I wrote got you hurt."

After a while, Ardella reaches over to touch Rachel's cheek. "The Ability," she says at length. "We have the Ability."

"That's even more horrible to think about. I'm going to quit. I don't want to live that way." Seated at the edge of her fold-away bed, casting her eyes about the small room, she begins rocking back and forth. "I only did it to get an education."

Rachel's laughter begins in a slow cadence. By the time it builds to a crescendo, Ardella is drawn along in its slipstream in spite of herself.

"All right," Ardella asks at length, "what's so funny?"

"No matter what they tell you," Rachel says, "no matter what inducements they offer, you must never, ever join their alumni association."

Absent Friends

Sam Zachary had six cans of Cat Chow Dinner Medley in his shopping cart when he paused to examine the lamb kidney in the meat counter. He found a small package that agreed with him and took it as well. Farther down the aisle, he made for the area where the chickens were displayed. With Paula coming for dinner, chicken would be ideal; so would the lamb kidney be fitting for Count Basie.

His lover and cat provided for, Zachary wheeled with satisfaction toward the wine display, where he saw Paula, steering a cart of her own. Her smile of recognition when she saw him, and his more detailed awareness of how she was dressed, opened the floodgates of erotic responses toward her.

Although she was not tall, Paula's limbs seemed a bit long for her torso. She wore a sleeveless A-line of moire silk with pastel splashes. Zachary had never seen her chestnut-colored hair grown long, had not known her until after the chemotherapy had sent the cancer scurrying for cover. Now her hair had grown back, shot through with gray. She kept it short because Zachary liked it that way, but also as a reminder of the difference between then and now. The innocence of invincibility, she'd said, and the mischief of the possible.

"Seduction dinner," Zachary grinned, inclining his head toward his intended purchases.

"Not necessary, kiddo. Already seduced." But when she

43

wheeled her own cart next to his to consolidate their selections, the pleasure of discovery that they'd chosen almost the same items was broken when she saw the cans of Cat Chow Dinner Medley and the lamb kidney. "Goddamn it, Sam. Why do you do this to yourself?"

"Hope," Zachary said. "Hope springs eternal in the breast of man."

"Denial. You have to learn to move on to the next plateau, whatever it is." While they stood in line at a checkout stand, Paula linked her arm through his. After a moment, she leaned her head on his shoulder. "I know how much you love him— and how much he loved you. But he's not coming back. Whatever the reason. Whether it was from accidental causes or maybe he decided it was time to go off and die. Animals seem to understand that need. They do it with such style."

"He's only six. That's hardly the age for a cat to start checking out hospices."

"Not everyone gets to live the span projected for them. I know it sucks, particularly if life seems to be going so well. Sometimes there are unanticipated events. Sometimes—" she seemed to consider for a moment, "—sometimes you have to make choices."

They fell silent for a time, reading the pronouncements of doom, betrayal, and tragedy on the front pages of the tabloids. Zachary was arrested by the headline, "Messy Rock Star Divorce—Battle Over Family Dog."

"Maybe someone took him," Paula said. "He'd rather be with you than anyone. If he could have come back, he would have."

"Ah, yes," Zachary said. "Zen detachment by the numbers." Aware that the young couple ahead of them in the line was watching, Zachary lowered his voice. "'Grant me the serenity to accept what I cannot change and the wisdom to know the difference.'"

"It worked for me, Sam. It got me where I am today. It's still working."

"Sure." He became aware of the young couple again. "And people like Copernicus, Jane Austen, and Beethoven all had the

44

wisdom to quit before pushing their talents to the limit, making this a safer place for democracy and the American dream."

Paula gave him a broad, farcical bump with her hip. "You are impossible, and I wish you'd take me to your home and make love to me with all deliberate speed."

The young man in front of Zachary turned to his mate with unabashed amazement. "Now that," he said, "is the way to have an argument."

"It only works," Zachary told him, "with the right woman—and the right cat."

— 🐾 —

Zachary lived in a mobile home park between the hilly out-reaches of Ortega Ridge just northwest of Summerland. Many of the mobile homes had an ocean or mountain view. From Zachary's perch, a hint of ocean could be had, but to get it, one would have to stand on the living room sofa or in the shower stall. Within Zachary's unit, there was room for an ambitious sound system and record collection, a larger-than-galley-sized kitchen, enough shelving for a great number of books. In addition to a bedroom of modest size, there was space for a small office work area.

Clad in a paisley robe that Paula had given him, Zachary addressed the matter of dredging pieces of chicken in a seasoned flour as she watched him from the dining table. "One of the perks of being my age," he said, "is the way you can rearrange priorities. Take your time with the ones you like. Give short shrift to the others. Just think, for example, how much better this coq au vin will be for our shuffling the order of things. Fifteen years ago, if I'd known you, I'd have strung out dinner, trying to get you into bed later."

"And now?"

"First things were first, dinner second."

Paula closed her eyes. "I was going to give you a cat tonight. I had it all picked out. Abyssinian."

Zachary drizzled olive oil into a large pan, which he set over

45

a low flame. "Right. A statement. 'Let go, Sam. Get on with life.'"

She shook her head. "More of a gesture. Of ongoing love."

"I shouldn't do this," Zachary said, mincing a clove of garlic into the pan. "Another perk of being older. You can put in garlic when you want. What changed your mind about the cat?"

"I got to thinking you'd love it because it was from me."

"What's wrong with that?" Zachary launched a piece of chicken into the pan, watched it with satisfaction.

"There should be a strong original chemistry between a person and a pet. Otherwise it gets to be, you know, custodial. Whenever you get the chance to love someone outside a custodial relationship, it seems to have more meaning."

"You make it sound like second-class citizenship to take care of someone."

"It isn't that. I happen to like the idea of having choices."

To the chicken pieces sautéing in the pan, Zachary added flame-roasted red peppers and a generous pile of diced shallots. "This has become a far cry from coq au vin."

Paula spoke with a pronounced laugh. "What we have always becomes a far cry from coq au vin. In fact, we never have had coq au vin."

"I should learn how to make pure, unadorned coq au vin."

"No," Paula said. "Please don't. Promise me you will never learn to make coq au vin."

"For reasons that evade me, this conversation has taken an ominous cast."

"How long will it take that concoction to cook?"

Zachary gave the pan a critical survey. "Forty minutes," he said. "Maybe forty-five. Why do you ask?"

"I was thinking how you always look so appealing when you wear that robe."

Zachary set down the spatula and lowered the flame under the chicken. "I may not be the virile young buck I once was," he said, advancing on her, "but if you want humorous love-making—I'm your man."

Paula stood to meet him. "That," she said, "is exactly what I want."

He awoke the next morning to the smell of fresh coffee and croissants in the warming oven. On the dining table, a large bunch of purple stock rested in a fluted pot he'd not seen before.

He confirmed his suspicions about the origin of the pot when he saw Paula's signature on the bottom along with the day and month—today's date—engraved before the firing process. The glaze contained her favorite colors, in many ways a replication of the dress she'd worn yesterday. This was the first time he'd known her to date a piece with such specificity. She was content to inscribe the year directly below her name. His birthday was not for another two months, nor was today any anniversary between them he could remember.

Her purse was not where she tended to leave it—on top of the bookshelf near the front door—but given the spontaneous intensities of last night, small wonder. He padded out to the parking area to see if her Toyota truck was still there. When he'd looked in its bed last night, her sleeping bag and small camping gear were stowed in the corner, signals of her intentions about a visit to her favorite area, up beyond Los Olivos toward Figueroa Mountain.

No truck.

On the way back, he paused to look under the foundation of his mobile home, recalling how, early in his association with Count Basie, the cat had indeed chosen to hide there once, whether in dedicated pursuit of some local lizard or in the service of some feline whim.

Down on his haunches, Zachary said, "You would tell me if you were in there—right?"

Back inside the mobile home, he poured more coffee, removed the croissant from the toaster, then found yet another surprise when he consulted the refrigerator for the container of peach chutney uppermost in his thoughts. Two large Mason jars of strawberry jam, Zachary's unquestioned favorite of all spreads, made by Paula, greeted him.

Spooning a generous blob of the thick jam into a dish,

Zachary settled down to a solitary breakfast with the morning newspaper and music from Public Broadcasting. He was midway through his second cup of coffee when he heard an insistent knocking at the door. At first his hopes flourished; it was the very sort of impatient knock Paula gave if she forgot her keys. But when he opened the door, he found a surprise of a different order than his discovery of the strawberry jam.

Before him stood Paula's daughter who, Zachary sensed, was in the throes of conflicting dramas currently resident within her. Even though she was much taller than Paula, Hillary was a tangible, incipient representation of her mother, sharp and angular in some places where Paula was rounder and softer, taut and impatient where Paula was limber and acceptant. There were neither frown lines on Hillary's generous brow nor were there laugh lines about her mouth. From behind hooded eyes and pouty lips there radiated a persistent and defiant sexuality.

"My timing is probably awful," she said, framing herself in the doorway, "but this is an awful time, isn't it?"

Zachary gestured her in.

"I know you think I'm a brat," she swept past him.

"Dramatic," Zachary said. "Sometimes to the point of theatricality. Have you had breakfast?"

"I can't eat when I'm all keyed up."

"That must make for interesting mealtimes with what's-his-name. Your husband?" Zachary produced a mug, filled it with coffee for Hillary.

"Stephen," she said.

"Right. Stephen. Your mother's jam. You're making a big mistake."

Hillary shook her head. "I've always envied people who could be calm at crisis moments." She flashed a sad smile. "One of the reasons I'm here is I wanted you to know I've left Stephen."

Zachary sipped at his coffee. "Why?"

"Because it just came to me. I'd only married him in the first place to get out of the house. Mom and Dad were beginning to come apart then, and I couldn't stand it. Their silences were awful. I kept thinking of Mom's and your silences. There was always something going on between you, even when you weren't talking. It was like watching silent conspiracies."

Zachary rose to get two more croissants. "I meant, why did you want me to know?" He pushed a dish with jam, croissant, and a knife toward her.

"So you can see that I have some understanding of the consequence of my actions." She tore a croissant apart and began applying jam. "Of all the men in my life, you're the only one who disapproves of me in a positive way."

"I wouldn't exactly say I was in your life."

She smiled in what impressed Zachary as a rueful manner, one of the few times he'd seen her so reflective. "I know it's none of my business, but I always wondered why you and Mom never married. You seemed so good for each other. I'd watch you two together and I'd be jealous. Then I'd go home and be bitchy. Ah, poor Stephen." Hillary surprised Zachary when she reached across the table to squeeze his hand, a gesture that included more than the usual sexuality in which she wrapped so many of her attitudes, and which contained as well the sense of what seemed like conspiracy between them. At first Zachary was irritated until he realized what Hillary meant to convey: a sense of shared secret that was not at all conspiratorial. "It's true," she said. "I've come to get some comforting and approval. But I'd also like to remedy the part about you not being in my life."

Zachary was distracted from his attempts to sort things out by a rustling sound at the door. "The disapproving but wise father figure, is that it?"

"I really wrestled with coming here, Sam. I thought of all number of things. Interventions. Emergency measures. Things I could do on my own. I thought—"

"You thought—"

"I thought we were through with the uncertainty."

By the time Zachary reached the door, the rustling sound turned into a persistent cadence of bumping, as though someone with an armload of packages were using a hip or elbow as a substitute for knocking. Or, as Zachary discovered when he opened the door, as a medium-sized black cat with white spats, pushing at the door. "Well," Zachary said, standing aside with a flourish. "Well, well, well."

Count Basie, leaner than Zachary had last seen him, dusty and disheveled, moved inside, trailing a litany of meowed complaint in his wake.

Zachary started for the refrigerator, stopped, scooped the cat into his arms for a moment, before he set him on the dining table. "I'm glad you're back, old friend. Truly glad." An enormous sense of relief seemed to settle on him like a comfortable old jacket. He began humming as he brought forth the lamb kidney and the remains of last night's chicken. Only then did the soft, muffled sounds of Hillary's crying reach him. He turned to regard her.

"You don't know yet, do you, Sam? You have no idea what this is all about."

"You're bailing out on what's-his-name, and it's a bit scary, and maybe some of your feelings about me need sorting out."

Hillary wiped at her eyes with a napkin and shook her head. "You haven't been to the post office box to pick up your mail. You haven't got your letter from her yet, have you?"

Zachary spread his palms at these assertions.

"And now it works out that you're going to learn about it from me. I don't think she had it planned that way."

Zachary was aware of his cat, standing on the table, managing to purr at the same time he ate with such an avid concentration. He took in the details about him. Zachary's eyes met Hillary's and for the first time since he'd known her, he saw they were the same color as Paula's. "Maybe she did," he said.

The Man Within

Asher could not bear to face those assembled in the room although he knew, as he cast his eyes down, that his gesture would be mistaken for modesty. Let them think what they would. He feigned preoccupation with his notebook, cheeks smarting from the rush of blood.

"Our congratulations to Mr. Asher," Ms. Cash said. "His triumph is a lesson to all of us."

"A story," Naomi Bloom said. "A story would have been better. There's something elegant, even noble about a story."

Asher winced.

Ms. Cash stepped from behind the lectern smiling and assured, her paisley scarf a jaunty reminder of her good taste. "I agree with you, Mrs. Bloom. A story is a wonderful form, but the essay is no less valid a literary creation—and Mr. Asher does have a poetic turn of phrase. Which publication is it, Mr. Asher, that has accepted your article?"

He could not bring himself to look at Ms. Cash. "*The*—"

"Speak up, please, Mr. Asher."

"*The Tri-Counties Senior's Reader.*"

When Ms. Cash nodded, she presented a fine jaw line that Asher had heard many of the women in the group describe with envy. "Please bring in a copy when it appears. I'll post it on the bulletin board so everyone who comes to Casa Jocasa Senior Citizens' Center is able to see what fine work our writing group does."

"*The Tri-Counties Senior's Reader*," Naomi Bloom said. "Isn't that one of those throw-away papers?"

"They give good two-for-one restaurant coupons," Ira Blau said.

"You have to wonder about their taste," Naomi Bloom said. "It's a far cry from *The Paris Review*."

Ms. Cash spread her hands. "I think," she said, "this is a good time for a break."

— ❧ —

Treating himself to a coffee at the Golda Meir honor bar snack shop, Asher was trying to fend off congratulations from some of his classmates and regain a semblance of composure when Ira Blau appeared, his owlish eyes refracting admiration through thick glasses with somber black frames. Blau's grin was bigger now than when Asher, counting on Blau's inability to keep a hold on exciting information, had told him about the acceptance by *The Tri-Counties Senior's Reader.*

"You old finesser," Blau said. "Don't ever try to get me into a card game with you."

"What finesser?"

"I see right through your stratagem, Asher. You used me. You got me to tell Ms. Cash. That way, it wouldn't seem like it was coming from you." He winked. "All in the noble cause of love. For that I don't mind."

Asher watched him, noncommittal. He took a sip of coffee. Could he have underestimated Blau?

"From the very beginning, your plan worked. How can you be so calm about it now? She practically threw herself at you. Did you see how she stood up for you? Only a fool could fail to recognize—"

"Blau, what are you talking about?"

"Janet Cash. Your plan to enlist her sympathies, your plan to—You are a very devious man, do you know that?"

"And you," Asher said, "are a lunatic. Cash is married."

"As my grandchildren are fond of reminding me, this is a new century we're living in."

52

"Cash is happily married. You're so smart, you understand what 'happily married' means, Blau? And even if she were interested, I have twenty, twenty-five years' head start on her."

Blau shook his head. "I didn't realize she was so old." Then his eyes blinked in recognition. He took a gulp of air. "A day late and a dollar shy, but now I get it." His voice rose with excitement. "Naomi Bloom." He clapped his hands. "Va-va-va Bloom."

Asher grabbed for Blau's collar, missed, and grabbed again for his arm. "I swear it, Blau, if you say so much as a word to her—if you say a word to anyone—"

"You're not interested in Ms. Cash at all, it's Naomi Bloom you did this for."

— 🐝 —

At his first sight of Naomi Bloom, Asher set down the coffee he had been drinking at one of the three window tables at Langer's Bakery and Deli. He grabbed at his chest as though he had been wounded. Indeed, Kroll, who had a small office in the same building as Asher, and with whom Asher now sat engaged in a game of chess, was moved to ask if the problem was with Asher's heart.

"It may well be." Asher moved to the door and thrust forth into the sunny late afternoon in the direction Naomi Bloom had taken toward the upper part of Milpas Street, where ethnic diversity and small mom-and-dad ventures such as Langer's had begun to lose out to the encroachment of urban renewal.

A short woman—Asher guessed five three—with shiny auburn hair wound into a shape reminding Asher of a round knotted loaf of egg bread, Naomi Bloom exuded purpose, striding with shoulders back, head at a defiant angle.

Asher had not the slightest notion what he would say to her, only that he must say something. Perhaps it would be to explain to her that an area of himself of which he had at best a scanty knowledge had seemed to open up at the sight of her as she passed the window of Langer's in an A-line dress worn over black Danskin tights, bright violet socks, and an equally intense pair of pink Reebok aerobic shoes.

But even this inchoate strategy was doomed by Asher's discovery that Naomi Bloom had been fast enough to move beyond his vision.

He waited for several moments, hoping to see her emerge from one of the shop fronts. After a time, some inner voice told him his quest was hopeless, and the voice of Willie Langer wondered at some volume, "Asher, you want I should put your unfinished Danish in the refrigerator until tomorrow?

Dispirited, Asher returned to his table and sank into his chair. "Tell me I wasn't dreaming."

"You weren't dreaming." Kroll moved his knight to a point where he had a particularly powerful fork on two of Asher's key pieces. "That was the answer. What was the question?"

"That woman who passed. I don't know when I've ever seen a more remarkable woman. She made me realize something I'd completely overlooked."

Kroll grinned. "Speaking of overlooked—" He used his strategic knight to take Asher's rook. In celebration, he swirled the last of his cheese Danish into his coffee and plunked it in his mouth. "You mean Naomi Bloom?"

"That's her name? Naomi?"

Chewing, Kroll nodded.

"Is she married?" Asher brought up his own knight to take a pawn.

"Not a very good exchange, a pawn for a rook. So. Naomi Bloom. She made you realize you are a man?"

Asher felt his face redden. "What's wrong with that? By the way," he said, "that's mate in three moves."

Kroll studied the board, swore when he realized the inevitability. "A cholera on you," he said. Then he said, "She's in her mid-fifties."

"But her body is like forty-five."

Kroll dabbed at his jowl with a paper napkin. "A widow. At least three years. He was some overachiever from L.A." His eyes flickered with revenge. "A CPA. His ticker gave out."

"Not all accountants are Type A personalities," Asher said.

"Is that so?" Kroll nodded. "Okay, you give me a fact, so I'll

54

return the favor. Mind you, I have no first-hand information, but there are reasons to believe she has a lover."

"This calls for a celebration." Asher motioned to Willie Langer for fresh coffees and baklavas for himself and Kroll, who began shaking his head, not at being stood a round of coffee and pastry but at the larger issue. "I don't get it," he said. "He comes down here in his usual lugubrious fashion for a game of chess. In the space of minutes, he sees the woman of his dreams, he learns she may already have a lover, and he's suddenly pleased with life."

Asher made a dismissing gesture. "Competition is nothing to me. It's the opportunity I'm interested in."

He began to spend more time at Langer's, hoping for another glimpse of Naomi Bloom, at first lingering over his coffee and *Wall Street Journal,* then lapsing into handwritten correspondence with a favored nephew at the Wharton School of Business, and finally extending to first drafts of tax forms or business plans for clients.

While he waited for the reappearance of Naomi Bloom, Asher even began to skim volumes from a Great Books by Correspondence course he'd enrolled in, underlining passages with relevance for him in a bright yellow highlighting pen and making notes in his crabbed Spencerian hand on the backs of old ledger sheets.

This could all have been done from his apartment, the master bedroom of which had been furnished with a long table from Cost Plus Imports and numerous shelves and institutional chairs from a used school-furniture shop in Ventura. But going to an office was the habit of a lifetime. While clients seemed to come to him rather than his seeking them, Asher was still not at the stage where he could with comfort pursue life from his residence.

The one time Asher remained in his office to work on a quarterly tax report, Naomi Bloom actually entered Langer's, directing Willie to a complex order of sandwiches and salads. Asher arrived just in time to see her leave, her purchases thrust into two net bags from which protruded the necks of wine bottles, a long loaf of French bread, and bright splotches of Gerbera daisies.

From this circumstantial evidence Asher knew with a jealous ache that Naomi Bloom was going to meet her lover.

He set forth at a discreet distance as she moved toward the industrial tract on lower Milpas, puzzled by her destination until he realized there was a shortcut across undeveloped flatlands and railroad sidings, leading to Cabrillo Boulevard and the beach. The trouble with following her, even at a great remove, was the openness and a lack of other persons on foot, inviting her suspicion if not outright discovery if she should see him.

Torn between his interest in watching the rhythmic undulations of her hips and his curiosity at seeing the man whom she was going to meet, Asher shortened his stride and tried to feign interest in the railroad tracks, as if to legitimatize his presence and dilute a degree of the prurience from his purpose. After some time, he saw a man of about his own height emerging from behind a windowless tar-papered shed, then set off on a course that would intercept Naomi Bloom.

Asher felt stirrings along the lower regions of his spine. Even though it was impossible for the intruder to see with any exactitude the contents of the string bags Naomi lugged, it was easy for Asher to imagine the man, probably one of the street people or transients who frequented the area, seeing Naomi's bags as a target of opportunity. Stepping up his pace, Asher moved forth with the adrenalined certainty of a confrontation. The man was on a collision vector with Naomi. Asher set forth, thrilled with the thought that he would formally meet her as her rescuer. The man wore a duckbilled cap. A formless khaki jacket flapped behind him. He called out to Naomi Bloom, who stopped in her tracks, turning to face him, letting the bags slip from her hands as she extended her arms.

When Asher saw this, a shard of agony flashed through him like a crackle of lightning on a summer evening. This was no goddamned assault on Naomi, no street person literally stealing groceries from a helpless widow; this was Naomi Bloom's lover, clasping his arms about her waist, his hands now taking large bold portions of those very buttocks Asher had not long before begun to admire.

The sight of Naomi Bloom with the man in the duckbilled cap told Asher much of what he wanted to know about her but more than he was able to bear with calmness. He turned away from them, sat on the sun-cracked adobe soil, removing an imaginary rock from his shoe, looking over his shoulder at what he considered appropriate intervals to see if they had parted from their greeting.

After several minutes, the couple was underway again, each carrying in their outer arm one of the bags of provender for the picnic, their inner arms wound about each other.

Asher replaced his shoe and set forth after them at a careful distance as they headed for Cabrillo Boulevard and the park extending along the beach, thinking the site for the picnic might be at one of the wooden plank tables scattered in the area beyond the volleyball courts. He soon realized they meant to continue around the slope of foothill directly west of the old cemetery to one of the many small, secluded coves between the cemetery and the Biltmore Hotel.

The man who could spot Kroll the smaller triumph of his knight fork in order to engineer a larger plan, Asher moved out onto Channel Drive, then took the steep road up past the front of the cemetery, arriving at the crest of the hill from which he could see the ocean. More important, he had a good view of the coves on the beach below and a place to watch from which he had little likelihood of being seen.

Turning up the collar of his thin sports coat, Asher settled in to watch the sun, hurrying to its nadir over the section of Santa Barbara called the Mesa, and to wait for the two picnickers.

When the lovers came into view, they continued to clasp each other about the waist, a fact that was beginning to give Asher pangs of jealousy, until it became apparent they were not in agreement about the precise site for the picnic, the man wanting a large segment of conglomerate that had once been a wall somewhere and had years since been dumped here as a breakwater to protect the hill above them against ravages of incoming tides.

Naomi wanted a spot farther back, where they could lie in

the sand. Asher was beginning to think he would have sided with her.

A compromise was reached at a spot agreeable to both of them as a half-way mark. The man spread a large cotton blanket. After Naomi placed the Gerbera daisies in an empty bottle, she began removing from a series of small containers the feast Willie Langer had prepared. Using a corkscrew on his knife, the man opened a bottle of wine, then poured two paper cups. When he handed one to Naomi and tipped his against hers, she grew playful and knocked off his cap, again inciting Asher's jealousy. How grand it would be to have a woman who, in play, would swipe off your cap. When he saw how Naomi's lover combed his long bushy sidelocks to cover an advanced stage of male-pattern baldness, Asher felt more charitable considering his own less pronounced bald spot and receding hairline.

He settled in to wait, not precisely sure what he was waiting for. A growl in his stomach reminded him that whatever it was he sought to discover, he would be better able to cope with it if he had one of Willie Langer's roast beef sandwiches on thick rye bread, with Russian dressing. The secret, of course, was a layer of coleslaw between the bread and meat.

As the sun continued its downward arc and caused long shadows, Asher watched in mounting fascination as Naomi and her lover, seated close together, exchanged bits of the feast and sipped wine. At one point, they playfully tossed olive pits first at each other and then at marauding curlews and godwits. Asher understood from this that they were waiting for some semblance of darkness to arrive in which to make love. Chess games were sorry excuses for such gambits as these.

Now he was faced with moral and aesthetic dilemmas—whether to stay or leave before the onset of their activity expanded from its current culinary foreplay.

His first attack at the problem came in the form of closing his eyes, imagining it was he who was now dining with Naomi Bloom, his insensitivities being assuaged instead of those of the semi-bald man. This approach became so successful that Asher was undone. Leaning back against the sheltering side of his perch, offering Naomi Bloom a dream-cast Kalamata olive, which she put between her teeth and then dared him to remove without, of course, the use of his hands, he promptly fell asleep.

Asher underwent the hazy erotic sleep of a man transfixed, bewitched, entombed in his own needs. He was aware of the fall of darkness and the distant tinkle of laughter mingled with the cackling sound of the retreating tide, skittering over a floor of small rocks.

The membrane of Asher's sleep was broke at the sense of the celebration below being over. A new, resident attitude—anxiety—seemed to stomp metaphorical sand from its metaphorical feet. Asher opened his eyes, for the moment disoriented, knowing only that he was cold and hungry. A woman's voice came out of the darkness behind him. "If I miss that bus—"

A man's answer was gruff and indistinct.

"It's you and your overweening pride," the woman countered. Asher stood rooted to the spot when Naomi Bloom stormed by, not twenty-five feet away, her wispy hair bedraggled. The man with the duckbilled cap chuffed after her, lugging the remains of the picnic. They crossed the Channel Road, heading toward the bus stop.

"I shouldn't have to put up with this, Harvey," Naomi Bloom said. "I get it from you on one side and the kids on the other. I'm too old for this kind of game. I shouldn't have to sneak home. I should be able to come and go as I please."

At first, Asher could not make out the man's response. Whatever it was, Naomi Bloom, who could make it out, took exception. "What?" She said, turning on the man. "What did you say?"

Asher, positive she was looking directly at him, sought refuge in the shadow of a tree.

"I wondered," the man said, "if you thought you were some kind of Emma Goldman with your goddamn independence."

"That's what I thought you said." Naomi Bloom wrested a string sack from him and extracted a flute of French bread, which she brandished, swordlike, advancing at him. "Mr. G. Harvey Bigshot has his own car, but can he use it to take his girlfriend home?"

"Calm down, Naomi. Just calm down."

"Fuck calm down."

"There's no need to talk that way. The car is my home. I don't drive it, I sleep in it. I *work* in it."

"Fuck you. Fuck your car. I'll talk any way I fucking please." With the flute of French bread, Naomi poked the man in the sternum. "I can't live like this anymore," she said, "and stop telling me to calm down. You always tell me to calm down. If you're so interested in a calm girlfriend, go find one and let *her* take the bus home." She said this as the bus growled up the grade, then veered in toward the curbside at her signal.

"You'll come around," the man said as Naomi Bloom boarded the bus. "Mark my words. Two, three days without, you'll be happy to see me."

Naomi Bloom swept her skirt about her and boarded the bus, pausing in the entry well. "So for two, three days, I'm a free woman. Get lost, Harvey."

The bus whisked away, accelerating up the grade as Naomi Bloom's lover stood in its wake, muttering to himself, then declaiming to the cosmos. "Ungrateful broad. You'll rue the day."

Standing in the shadows, Asher was tempted to answer on her behalf.

— ❦ —

The next day, Asher was at Langer's, pantomiming a description of Naomi Bloom, asking impulsive questions about her in a manner uncharacteristic of him—incomplete sentences. "That woman. Yesterday. The picnic. Naomi Bloom."

Willie Langer gave a broad wink while folding spindly arms on the deli counter. "It is said she lives with her children."

"This is not an exercise in Talmudic argument. Where does she live with her children?"

"You want to deliver her next picnic, is that it?"

"Goddammit, Langer."

A look of confidentiality came into his face. "Well, I tell you, Asher. A clever man like you, he could probably make important discoveries at the Casa Jocasa."

"That's—that's a senior citizens' center."

"You see," Willie Langer smiled. "Already you have learned something."

Half an hour later, Asher was in the Casa Jocasa, a large cinder- block building with a thick coat of Navajo white paint, numerous trellises, flowerpots, and other indifferent or whimsical attempts to somehow look like part of Santa Barbara's Spanish heritage. After paying a birdlike woman with close-cropped hair four dollars, Asher was given a Casa Jocasa membership card and led to a large bulletin board which bore a hand-lettered sign, activities. Here he soon discovered that Naomi Bloom was indeed a member, enrolled in the Tuesday night Great Books of the Western World Discussion Group and the Thursday night Creative Writing Group.

He bought a spiral-bound notebook and a copy of *The Poetry of Robert Browning*, both of which he carried as props that first Thursday night. Freshly barbered, wearing neat khaki pants, a checked shirt that had been steamed into submission, and a gray herringbone jacket, Asher took the added measure of applying Lilac Vegetal aftershave.

The writing group met in the David Ben-Gurion room, which may have been the living room of the residence that had become Casa Jocasa. Asher arrived early and stood about the entryway, hopeful of being able to sit next to Naomi Bloom and make an auspicious beginning. But when Janet Cash called the class to order promptly at seven, Naomi Bloom had yet to arrive. Asher was drawn to the front by Janet Cash so that she could introduce him to the others. He was placed next to Ira Blau. An empty chair remained on Asher's other side, but it was soon taken by Mitzi Berlin. Well after Asher's introduction, Naomi Bloom swept into the room and settled noisily into a seat in the rear as Ms. Cash was commending the so-called little or literary magazines to the attention of the class.

Asher strained to listen, sensing that others as well were interested in the thrust of Ms. Cash's commentary, but a rather persistent grumbling—or was it muttering?—seemed to become a counterpoint, issuing from the rear of the room. Mitzi Berlin puckered her face in distaste and hissed for quiet. "The literary critic," Mitzi Berlin whispered to Asher. "Always with the comments."

"Who?" Asher mouthed the word.

"You're new. You'll see," Mitzi Berlin nodded.

"I think it might be helpful," Ms. Cash said, "if we all stood, took a few deep breaths, and stretched."

Mitzi Berlin sneered. "A minor in psychology. You can always tell." When she saw Asher was puzzled, she explained. "The teachers they send here, regardless of the subject, you can always tell when they minored in psychology. Whenever there's a disagreement or someone asks an embarrassing question, they want you to stand up and stretch. Unkefer from the ceramics class? A psychology minor. Conrad from life drawing? A psychology minor. Only Lynds from Szechwan cooking and Shelton from Exploring the Film Noir don't make you get up and stretch."

During the break, Asher approached Naomi Bloom, his heart aflutter as he introduced himself. This was as close as he'd been to her; wisps of auburn hair fell in random array about her angular face. Her eyes blazed more of a certainty and presence than a color. Her lips seemed ready to put stage directions into her every expression, and the crow's feet at the sides of her eyes struck him as traces of resident bouts of laughter.

"Howard Asher," she said. "Big deal."

Now, Asher was positive he was in love. He noticed flecks of grass on her skirt. It had been four days since her picnic with the man in the duckbilled cap.

After what he had already begun to think of as The Debacle, Asher sought to buffer the sting of his misdirected debut as an author by going to Riparetti's, a neighborhood bar near the Casa Jocasa. Some solace was due. Not even Naomi Bloom's approaching him after class had a positive effect.

"I should not let personal attitudes influence my response to your news of publication," she told him. "I am undergoing what you might call the trauma of withdrawal and I lashed out at the closest thing. I am an emotional woman, yes—but not inconsiderate."

At Riparetti's, Asher cursed his own shortsightedness. Why had he not invited her for a drink? Why had he not asked her about her own reasons for taking Ms. Cash's class?

"Was that yes or no to another drink?" the bartender asked above the blare of a jukebox loaded with the Latino equivalent of Country Western.

"What?" Asher said.

"Yes, sir. One Coors, coming up."

Asher did not want the next beer. Nor did he want the three others to follow, but the litany of complaint about his failure to recognize splendid opportunities served to blunt his defenses to their arrival. Midway through the last beer, it came to Asher that a course of action was still open. The seven-block walk to the residential area where Naomi Bloom lived with her son, his wife, and their children did nothing to blunt his resolve and, in fact, gave him the opportunity to try out his gambit in the intimacy of the chilly, overcast night, giving his voice a husky cast.

Naomi Bloom lived in an older neighborhood, where mature stone pines and jacaranda buckled the sidewalk with their overgrown roots; yards with arbors, trellises, and rock gardens reflected idiosyncratic pride of ownership; it was also an area known for guest cottages or mother-in-law apartments, outbuildings added surreptitiously, even cynically, to produce extra rental income in a city gone mad over property values.

Shambling along Mason Street, Asher found the house he sought and moved by slowly to reconnoiter. A woody swath of flowering pear and oleander separated the house where Naomi lived from its neighbor. The ground was covered with granulated cedar bark, leaves, and the needles from nearby pines. Asher darted for the cover of the oleander, pleased to note he made no crunch or other telltale noise. With the exception of a few lights in one of the front rooms, the main house was in darkness, but there, just beyond the garage was a small outbuilding. What might have been a night light glowed in the darkness. As Asher moved closer, he made out the somber excesses of the second movement to Tchaikovsky's symphony, the Pathetique.

It was a small building, probably one large room, a modular stall shower and toilet in some convenient corner, a modest closet, and the thing that would make it especially illegal in Santa Barbara—a small kitchen.

Asher scooped up a handful of cedar granules and tossed one at the window. With a speed that startled him, the door opened. Naomi Bloom appeared, framed in the dim light. She spoke in a whisper. "You've got a lot of nerve, coming here."

Asher brought his reply down to the same conspiratorial tone. "I had to see you."

"Sure you did."

"You don't understand," Asher called across the night dampness.

"I understand plenty. It's seven, eight days. The shoe's on the other foot. Now you're the one with the itch. I've told you. No more. I'm free of you. I don't look back."

Asher tried to inject a plaintive, needful note. "I'm not who you think I am."

"Who among us is what the other thinks? I got that right out of the used-book store edition of Sartre you gave me for my birthday, you cheap son of a bitch."

"It's Howard. Howard Asher."

Naomi Bloom broke all pretense at a whisper. "Oh, for Christ's sake."

A floodlight erupted into life at the rear of the main house. "Mama," a reedy male voice called. "Are you all right?"

"Quick," Naomi Bloom whispered. "Get in here." She opened the door and stood aside. Asher burst from his cover. He reached the door in several strides, running low. As he passed Naomi, time seemed to suspend. He was aware of her hair, longer than he'd ever seen it; she wore a simple flannel gown, which had a faint smell of lavender.

He was not expecting a comfortable reading chair near the door nor its companion footstool, which tripped him. Asher crumpled in a heap, about six feet beyond her, on a large braided rug that skidded with his momentum. "I'm fine," Naomi Bloom called. "Nothing more than one of those radio call-in shows I like."

"You're sure, Mama?" the reedy voice persisted.

An edge came to her response. "I'm positive, Marshall." She paused for a moment to sigh. "Thank you for asking."

Asher clambered to his feet. Closing the door, Naomi Bloom turned to him, giving him the same critical scrutiny she used when considering the purchase of a Sabbath chicken. "What are you doing here, Asher?"

Before he could answer, she shook her head. "Ahh, I know what you're doing here." A dismissive wave of the hand. "It won't work. I've already been married to you—and you died, three years ago. Why should I make the same mistake with you again?"

"I'm not the same," Asher said. "I swear it."

"An accountant, no?"

"An accountant, yes, but different. I'm not compulsively neat. I like modern music. I take risks."

When Naomi Bloom hooted, Asher advanced, reaching for her hand. "That man with the duckbilled cap. Are you really through with him?"

Naomi yanked her hand free. "What do you know about him?" She made for the edge of the hide-a-bed, protruding from the sofa like an extended tongue. She sat, seemed to consider this was an invitation for him to sit next to her, rose, and made for the reading chair.

"I followed you."

Naomi laughed, but Asher was enough pained by its ironic note to know it was not the combustive laughter of conciliation.

"Why me?" she said.

"I don't completely understand it yet, myself."

"I'm not asking you," Naomi Bloom snapped. "I'm asking the cosmos. You think you're Mr. Different? My husband followed me until he wore me down. That man? With the duckbilled cap? G. Harvey Prell, he followed me, sometimes with tears in his eyes until I gave my heart to him. Do you know who he is?"

Asher shook his head.

"No, of course you don't. That's the way he wants it—nobody knows but me."

Taking a canvas-backed director's chair from the small dining table, Asher sat, fascinated as Naomi Bloom spoke of Prell's one hundred sixty-seven appearances in literary and quality magazines with short stories of bitter, minimalistic irony, of his fabled reputation, already causing printed speculation from the academics. "He signs himself G. Prell. The G is for Gershon, but using just the letter like that makes him feel a kinship to B. Traven."

"I'm sorry." Asher asked.

"I'll give you this, Howard Asher. You're honest. B. Traven was a writer, a secretive, misanthropic man who valued his privacy above all else." She paused for a long sigh, examining her bare feet as though there were some existential instructions for happiness printed on them. "Sometimes when Prell had too much wine, he would—"

"Yes?"

"He would put his head in my lap and tell me he felt like he is the Jewish B. Traven." She spoke of Prell's past. "Once he owned a chain of motels, all up the coast. Ventura, San Luis Obispo. Atascadero. Monterey. A wife and three children. Then he read *The Moon and Sixpence*. The character Charles Strickland, who was based on the painter Gauguin, you understand, spoke to him, and then Harvey knew what he must do. Now he lives in a black 1978 AMC Pacer. He types his stories on a manual typewriter he found in a pawnshop." She watched Asher with suspicion. "My husband felt an ideological affinity for John Maynard Keynes. Who speaks to you, Howard Asher?"

"You do." Asher was suddenly aware of bright light from the outside, and the voice of Naomi Bloom's son.

"Mama, is everything okay?"

Naomi Bloom shook her head. "How can anyone say there is no ruling force in the universe when there are sons who feel the need to do this one or more times a night? How can anyone speak to the randomness of nature when, of all the possible choices available to him, my son marries a woman named Ruth?"

"Are you all right, Mama?"

Naomi Bloom pointed to the small two-door closet near the stall shower. "In there," she said.

Asher took refuge in a darkness suffused with a combination of cedar fumes, lavender sachet, and a musky aroma that was probably pure Naomi Bloom, given off from her clothing. He was aware of the pounding of his heart and the sounds of his own breathing. A wave of excitement spread over him.

"Well, Marshall, now what is it?"

"Ruth was worried."

"Only Ruth, not you?"

"We want you to be happy."

"Do you have any idea what it would take to make me happy, Marshall?"

"Look, Ma, I know things haven't been easy for you since Dad died—"

"That's what you think? That's all? How about this? How about my having a life of my own with friends of my choosing?"

"A trip. They have these lovely seniors cruises you take with people of like interests. Alaska. The fiords of Norway."

Naomi trumpeted scorn. "A seniors tour to some godforsaken place, jammed in with a bunch of old barracudas who line up an hour early for the buffet?"

"It's important to keep active at your age."

"Marshall, it comes to me that you are torn by the ambivalence of wondering if I have a gentleman friend hiding under the bed and hoping that I don't. For God's sake, Marshall, set Freud to rest."

"Mama, that's not fair."

"I'll show you fair. Here, look."

Asher heard the sound of springs compressing and realized Naomi Bloom was lifting the hide-a-bed.

"There. No one. You see? No one. Now please go back to your earnest wife and your concerned children and tell them I am safe and secure, maintaining a healthy interest in my surroundings thanks to the miracle of talk radio. I am even thinking of raising tropical fish, taking up lawn bowling, and possibly knitting or crocheting."

"Mama, that wasn't necessary."

During an awkward silence, Asher became fearful his breathing would be heard. In the close, fragrant excitement of Naomi Bloom's closet, he had a protracted sense of embracing her in the darkness.

"Mama, what is it? Why are you looking that way?"

"You're absolutely right," Naomi Bloom said. "None of this is necessary. I shouldn't be doing this, not any of it. I should be my own person in surroundings of my own choosing."

"When Dad died we agreed—"

"You agreed. You and your brother and sister agreed—and in what I thought was my grief, I let you do it."

"Mama, there's no need to shout. Everything is all right."

Naomi Bloom laughed. "Have I got news for you, sonny boy. Sit down. For this, you'll need to sit down. No? You won't sit down? Then take your enlightenment standing up." Her voice raised. "Asher, you can come out now."

Asher froze, wondering if any future with Naomi was at stake on this cast of her whim. Should he emerge now or let her play out her gambit?

"You've made your point, Mama. I'm going now."

"Marshall, I am deadly serious. At this very moment there is someone in my closet, a man named Howard Asher, who has an enormous erection and who wishes to become my lover."

From the darkness, Asher erupted in a grin. He neatened the set of his corduroy jacket, then stepped out of the closet. After a few blinks to accustom his eyes to the brightness, he nodded respect at Naomi Bloom and acknowledged her son. "Howard Asher," he said. "You are probably wondering why I asked you here this evening."

Molly

Late one spring night, during a satisfying buffet and agreeable conversation at one of Reeva and Jerry Zachary's gatherings, Lessing understood with an ardent certainty that he intended to steal their dog, Molly, and somehow contrive to rear her as his own.

A six-year-old mixture of Cattle Dog and Australian Shepherd, Molly's coat was distinctive with its broad splotches of black and brindle, which gave the impression of the detail maps seen in the political section of Sunday newspapers. Thanks to an accident with a pair of hedge trimming shears, her tail was preternaturally short. Her bark, a crisp yip that evoked comparison with a coyote, marked her even further. To compound the problem, Lessing and the Zacharys had many acquaintances in common; short of boarding the dog out every time he had guests, what precautions could Lessing take to insure against eventual discovery? Added to these impediments, Jerry Zachary, a friend of Lessing's since university days, had the habit of dropping in on Lessing to drink pilsner beer and listen to Lessing's sound system.

Lessing had long enjoyed Molly, but it was a benign fondness; the impulse to steal her, to contemplate some kind of life with her, did not come until a conspiratorial bonding forged when he, almost directly behind Reeva Zachary's back, offered Molly a large shrimp from the scampi chafing dish on the buffet, and Molly, with a patrician nod of her head, took it. For the first time, Lessing sympathized with wealthy collectors who owned stolen works of art or kept archeological contraband locked away where only they could see it. Knowledge that he could contemplate such a plan gave him a galvanic surge of excitement, causing him forget plans to bring his date, Cynthia, back to his apartment.

"Hey, I thought we were going to your place," Cynthia said after they left the Zachary gathering. Before Lessing could retrieve any lost equilibrium, she'd pushed matters over the edge of recovery. "I knew it. That horsy blonde in the pink dress and spike heels who came by herself. Spilled a big glass of wine. Whatshername."

"Alida," Lessing said. In truth he had been building to quite a nice lust for Cynthia and had not found Alida to his liking. But once again, the thought of stealing Molly from the Zacharys and the extent of the logistics the theft would require, especially after the fact, overtook him, and he waited a critical beat too long to reply.

Cynthia seized the interval. "Some men your age have to have Porsches or Lotuses; for others it's blondes with freckles and long legs." Cynthia, who was neither blonde, freckled, nor long-legged, had stark topaz eyes set in a bony, angular face that Lessing found compelling. She reached for the door of his car. "You don't have to park. I'll get out here."

"Would it do any good to tell you it's not what you think?"

"No," they both said in unison.

— ❧ —

"Ah, Mr. Lawson, come in." Dr. Plotnick greeted Lessing from the center of a small, bright room, where a stainless steel examination table stood like a pagan altar, surrounded by shelves in which were displayed exotic implements, bottles of medications, and enlarged drawings of fleas and ticks. An early Beethoven string quartet wove its way through expensive, wall-mounted speakers. "I see you're having trouble getting your little friend to come in." A short man with a round head, thinning black hair, and dark shadowy cheeks, which he probably had to shave twice a day, Plotnick squinted behind designer-frame glasses at the file folder. "Would you like some help bringing–" he scanned the folder again "–er, bringing, er, your little friend in?"

Lessing decided Plotnick was at great pains to order his office clothing from the catalogue of some outdoors clothier. But something about the man spoke to his spending little or no time in what could be considered outdoors, much less wilderness. He was a man of the urban indoor tennis court and health club, but his image of himself included lug-soled moccasins, forest ranger twill trousers, and a red plaid field shirt. His loosely knotted black knit tie seemed a grudging concession to formality. "We don't have a listing of the name, type, and breed of your friend."

"I intend to pay for a standard visit," Lessing said, "but I have come alone, and it might be more comfortable if we talked in your office."

Plotnick pointed a finger at him. "You're the one who called yesterday, aren't you? In all my years in this profession, I've never been asked a question like that."

"Well," Lessing said, "what can you do?"

"It depends on the breed, of course, but there is always the possibility of docking the tail and shaping the ears by trimming or implanting the equivalent of one of those collar stays."

"What would that do?"

"Give upright, prick ears to a dog with floppy ears." Plotnick began to give himself over to the challenge. "Say the animal is piebald; the coat can be dyed a single color. A single-colored animal could be mottled. I suppose a longhaired animal with a straight coat can be made curly and vice versa. We might do some dental work if the animal is middle-aged or older, and if the animal is overweight, a diet could help. But many of these things could become expensive and require frequent mainte-nance. The bigger question is why you would want to do such a thing in the first place."

"I'm looking at options," Lessing said.

71

"Options, is it? There are enough available dogs in the world without having to resort to subterfuge."

"Some dogs are more desirable than others."

"That's it," Plotnick scowled. "Divorce. Now I see why you're here. Pure selfishness. You don't want to share the animal as community property, so you come sneaking over to a hospital where you've never been before and aren't likely to be traced." He stole a quick glance at the file folder. "I have to congratulate you, Mr. Lawson. In a world where it's easy enough to distrust our elected officials, religious leaders, and financial advisors, you've managed to add an entire new layer of corruption to human behavior." He wrote something Lessing could not read on the file folder and tossed it on the examining table. "I want nothing to do with your contemptible subterfuge." A final connection came to him. "Your name isn't really Lawson, is it?"

"No," Lessing said, "but it's very close."

"Very close?" Plotnick advanced on him. "Very close? Listen, if you don't get out of here right now, I'm going to do something very physical to you."

— 🦴 —

Lessing began to compile a schedule of the Zacharys' comings and goings, which he hoped to supplement with research. He drew a weekly calendar on a sheet of paper and began by marking off in red what he believed to be Jerry's hours away from the house.

Brian, their oldest son, was living in Ashland, Oregon, trying to make progress as an actor, and could be regarded as on his own. A room was still kept for Ondine, their daughter who was in school at Berkeley, but the furnishings were less hers than things that had worked their way out of other rooms and thought suitable for guests. Because of Reeva's dual status as a real estate broker and devoted part-time student, her hours were more likely to be notional. Lessing colored these in with a blue marker. The times they were both away from the house, such as Thursday nights at the health club, Lessing coded in black.

From recalled conversations, observations, and what he hoped were shrewd extrapolations, Lessing worked rapidly, producing a chart that was more substantial than he'd thought possible. The completeness of it gave him a vision of the Zachary's he had not before considered. It was easy to see, for instance, that they merely affected leisure. Whether they knew it or not, they were over-programmed. They did not spend much time together, which must account for their biweekly gatherings and their alternate Friday nights out at dinner and a play or concert. Even so, the chart revealed, when Reeva and Jerry were together, they were alone on rare occasions.

Lessing was lost in the contemplation of what charting his own activities would reveal—a Lessing's Uncertainty Principle?—when the door chime sounded with the distinctive shave-and-a-haircut ring pattern of Jerry Zachary.

When Lessing opened the door, Molly bounded in front of Jerry Zachary, sniffed at Lessing, wagged her truncated tail, then made for the kitchen. "I can leave her in the car," Zachary said.

"She'll be fine here. There's goulash if she's hungry."

Zachary extended a six-pack of pilsner beer. "Goulash, eh?"

In the kitchen, Lessing drew water for Molly. He set out ceramic bowls for himself, Zachary, and Molly while Zachary poured beer and put slabs of sour dough bread in to toast. "She seems to like you," Zachary said.

"She's used to me."

"She's used to the maid, she hates the gardener. You she likes." After a moment, Zachary observed, "I find it hard to accept your not having a dog or a cat. You always had one or the other hanging around."

"There's some hot paprika for the goulash if you want. Hungarian."

"It looks like Reeva and I are going to be able to get away for a few days. I suppose we could board her. Reeva heard about a guy in the Valley named Plotnick who plays classical tapes for his guests. Top conductors: Dutoit. Haitynk. Solti."

"You want me to look in on her at your place, play her some Mahler? What about it, Moll, *das lied von der erde?*" Lessing put the goulash bowls, toast, and beer on a tray and carried it into his study. Molly followed Zachary, but once in the study stationed herself at Lessing's side.

"I was hoping," Zachary said. "I was hoping you'd keep her here."

"How about the Berlioz *Requiem* V"

"Sure. Berlioz is fine. Well, what do you say?"

Molly followed Lessing to the shelves where the records, discs, and tapes were stored.

— 🐾 —

"Excuse me, but isn't that the Zachary dog?"

Lessing suffered a pang of defensiveness for which he reproached himself when he looked up from his coffee and newspaper. After all, Molly was legitimately with him. He had every right to be enjoying the ambience of the outdoor portion of the Xanadu coffee shop that permitted Molly to sit at his feet, sniffing at afternoon scents borne on a mild breeze. "Molly, it is," he nodded, recognizing his inquisitor as he waited for the adrenalin to run its course.

She sat at his table without being invited, herself a bit fluttery. "Alida Jacobi," she said. "I met you at the Zachary's two weeks ago. You were with that very serious looking brunette."

"Cynthia," Lessing said, waiting for her to continue.

"Of course I knew Molly, she's quite distinctive. How could anyone who knew her have any doubts? But I'll be frank with you. I knew you were sitting her for the Zacharys and the moment I saw her here, I thought you'd be nearby, and the first thing that came to my mind was that dumb question I asked you."

Lessing tilted his chair back, surveying her. True, he had not been especially drawn to her at their first meeting, but his preoccupation with Molly had caused him to bungle things with Cynthia, and now, watching her, he began to suspect there might be some potential for karmic redress with Alida. She was dressed for a visit to the supermarket next to the Xanadu: faded denims with a green and blue silk scarf as a belt, a chambray work shirt with rolled sleeves, a washable sun visor to protect her freckled forehead and cheeks. There were splotches of dried paint on the shirt and another small splotch on the side of her nose. No earrings although her earlobes were pierced. No makeup. No jewelry except for an old Zuni necklace with thick turquoise beads and mother-of-pearl surfaces.

Leaning farther back in his chair, Lessing caught sight of her serviceable but stylish latticework sandals, and he bore in for a closer inspection of the feature that could easily seal Alida's fate, so far as he was concerned, karmic debt or no karmic debt. Let others complain about misshapen noses, a prognathous jaw, or thighs bloated with cellulite. Lessing had no use, no sympathy, for long toes. This was no double standard, either. Although he had toes suitable to his own precepts, he had long been aware that he would have sought surgical correction if the reverse had been true. Long toes in a woman he otherwise admired were warning signals to be obeyed, and the times he had gone against his dictum had turned out to be bad times.

"Did I get something on my foot?" Alida said.

"I was just looking to see if you had long toes."

She nodded as if this made perfect sense to her. "I'm considered to be articulate and at least well-coordinated if not graceful, but this is not easy for me, and it isn't going well, I can see that. From the moment Reeva Zachary suggested I might like you and then invited me to that open house to meet you, I've simply not been at my best."

They were silent until a waitress appeared, asking if Alida wanted to order anything. When her café au lait was brought, Alida, in the act of taking a sip, spilled a good deal of it. While Lessing was helping her sop up the puddle with tiny paper napkins, Alida asked him, "Can you come to dinner sometime this week?"

Someone in the nearby parking lot fired up a motorcycle. Molly, outraged by the noise, followed it from the lot out onto the street, yipping defiance in its wake. She returned as Jack, a butcher from the market, came out for his coffee break, bringing Molly a lamb shank bone which she propped delicately between her front paws and gnawed at with an elegant poise, her eyes closed in mindless enjoyment. Lessing watched her with a mindless enjoyment of his own.

"You're very fond of her, aren't you?"

Lessing was wrenched back into the moment with another surge of defensiveness. It would have been easier to contemplate the robbery of the nearby jewelry store or to plan some elaborate and questionable financial manipulation than it was to contemplate the theft of a dog. There were so many implications, things that could be remembered and pieced together to form a mosaic of guilt.

"She's a fine animal," he said, thinking a neutral observation would cover the tracks of his intentions. "What about Wednesday?"

Alida smiled into the remainder of her coffee. "That's a relief. I was afraid I'd blown it."

"Do you have any dogs?"

Alida shook her head.

"Any kids?"

Her laughter was like a firecracker going off inside a tin can. "You are a funny man."

"Notional," Lessing said. "I was a funny man when I was younger. Unintentionally funny."

"You've been behaving mysteriously for some time."

Reeva Zachary moved about Lessing's study, searching for things to be dusted, moved, or straightened. She lifted a heavy free-form marble paperweight that Thornley, the sculptor, had given him, a notable dust trap. But she replaced it without wiping it. "Is there something wrong? Are you in any trouble?"

Lessing shook his head.

"Even now you look—that's it—you look unsettled. Wistful. Painfully reflective."

"I'm not in any trouble."

"I know you sometimes manage large sums of money."

"But I haven't been tempted. I'm not going to suddenly disappear with my secretary. The Feds aren't going to come around asking you provocative questions that will make you think I've been leading a double life."

Reeva perched on the edge of his desk. "Is it something with Alida? She says you become abstracted at the strangest times." Lessing poured coffee for each of them from the Thermos decanter on his bookshelf. For a moment, they drank in silence.

According to Lessing's taste, Reeva was a handsome woman who weighed less now than when she and Jerry began dating. Her face had aged well, giving her the appearance of character or compassion or humor, depending on the moment's need. He had envied Jerry his early discovery of her and his persistence in courting her. Now he had come to the awareness that his interest in Alida had something to do with a similarity he saw between Alida and Reeva. Both women could be highly vexing but of course Alida'a ability to exasperate him was now predicated on the fact of their having become lovers. "That's quite a bill of particulars you've got on me," he said. "Mysterious. Unsettled. Wistful. Painfully reflective. Abstracted."

"How is your health?"

Lessing snapped his fingers. "Right. We forgot about that. Am I the victim of some disabling disease? Ought I to review my will? Ought I to get my house in order?"

Reeva kicked one of her Reeboks at Lessing. "You *could* use a maid. Meanwhile I'm going to gather up our dog, go to the market, and restock the house. Amazing how a vacation makes home cooking seem attractive. You would be welcomed for dinner tonight, with or without Alida."

Lessing sipped his coffee as Reeva pecked his cheek, crooked a finger at Molly, and started for the door. "Maybe a trip would be the thing to get you out of your funk. Get in your car and go someplace unplanned," she said. "Thank you for taking care of Molly."

There was some pleasure in the fact that Molly looked back at Lessing twice before following Reeva, but it was bittersweet pleasure at best. Molly's departure left him feeling strangely alone, and the connection he'd just made between Reeva and Alida left him uncomfortable as well. He went to the kitchen and brought out the ingredients for spaghetti carbonara but stopped short of breaking the eggs when he remembered that spaghetti carbonara was the first meal he'd made for himself when he'd moved into his new apartment after the divorce and also the very dish he had prepared for himself after a woman he'd been dating for six months suddenly broke a thin flute of French bread over his head, called him enigmatic and vexing, packed her things that had been accumulating in the bedroom closet, and stormed out.

He made instead a thick sandwich, fortified with onion, tomato, and lettuce, the kind that had to be eaten while standing over the kitchen sink.

Just before dark, Lessing sat in his car outside the Zachary's home in the hilly Riviera section of Santa Barbara, not entirely sure why he had come until he saw Molly, sniffing at a hedge two houses away. He whistled softly, saw Molly's ears prick, her head snap about. She came to him at a cobbly but efficient run.

When Lessing opened the door, Molly jumped inside with an effortless lift, seeming to encourage conspiracy. Firing up the engine, Lessing chucked Molly lightly under the jaw. "We're off," he said.

He headed west for a time, into the brightest part of the evening, well past Goleta toward Mariposa Reina and the Gaviota Beach camps, with no particular destination in mind. Molly sat on the front seat, sniffing at the rush of information that ran by her nose in the breeze of movement.

Reeva's suggestion of a trip had great appeal for him. Steinbeck had set forth with a poodle, of all things. He'd had a revitalizing experience and a book out of it. Nearly all the street people seemed to have dogs—more sensible dogs than poodles—and actually appeared to fare the better for it.

Now, he had the coastline on his left and a sense of purpose in front of him. The car, which Lessing had come to regard as being as idiosyncratic as he was, had never responded so well.

The notion of driving without a destination felt as good to him as he imagined Molly felt, her nose out the open window. He hummed a fragile harmony to an Oscar Peterson CD.

At a roadside stand, Lessing got them hamburgers with everything, which they ate with ceremony, parked in front of a grassy dune near the beach, conspirators in a spontaneous adventure.

It was some time before the thought of Jerry and Reeva yanked at Lessing like a dog who has overrun its leash. "A little bit longer, while we walk off dinner," he said, heading across the dune.

Shortly before ten o'clock, he returned to the Zachary's to let Molly out. When Lessing called the next day to apologize for missing dinner, Jerry Zachary said, "Damndest thing. You'd think our dog would be glad to see us after we'd been away, but she took off for three or four hours and came back covered with sand and had caramelized onions on her breath."

"You'll have to accept it," Lessing said. "She has a life of her own."

Witness Relocation Program

Sometimes Milan makes the effort, gets to the Xanadu Coffee Shop a little early so he can be the one who nails down the prime table outside. His dog, Roxie, is curled at his feet when they start showing up: Mike Barnet, the musician, often the first; then J.D. Wolfe, professor out at the university. Somedays this guy Burnaby, Conrad Burnaby; they all make jokes about him being a fence for stolen jewelry. Then Rifkin, used to own Weight Watchers franchises. They deadpan Milan how Rifkin may look all right, Ralph Lauren shirts, tassel loafers, but he's actually a slum landlord. Then maybe Gerry Keller shows up, only guy in the group who gives Milan the creeps.

Milan can't figure out what these guys have in common except they seem to hang out for morning coffee. They bring bones or scraps for Roxie, completely ignoring the fact that if Milan wanted to, he could spoil the dog rotten on his own, given the way he and Dale live.

Isn't as if they don't know who Milan is married to; you know anything at all about Milan, you have to remember the stink Dale's ex made when Milan started dating her. Talk about using the media. Every time you went to the supermarket, the tabloids yowling: "Steve Wells to John Milan: 'Give back my wife!'" Wells was technically her ex by then, but that's another story.

Even if these guys aren't the sorts who see the tabloids,

weren't they all here that morning a couple of months back when Dale comes here, practically hysterical, no shoes. Looking at her, you're thinking she's probably got nothing on under that robe and even if she has, she's a distraction because she looks so vulnerable, no make-up, her hair unbrushed. She marches right up to Milan. "Johnny," she gives, "you have got to come home right now and do something about that sonofabitch gardener." Doesn't say another word, goes marching right back to her Mercedes, and these guys, they don't make a big thing out of it. One of them even offers to walk Roxie.

And then, knowing as they do that he is with Dale, wasn't it Wolfe who gives him the nudge one morning as some woman in a sundress is going into Von's market—what a hoot. They call it Von's of the Stars because some show people shop there—to buy groceries. "'You have got to see this," Wolfe says. "A definite two-groaner."

"We have a grading system," Barnet says. "One groan being hearty approval, two being significant arousal, and three being the male menopausal ideal."

And Milan, turning to look at the woman, is thinking possibly a three before he comes out of it and realizes he really likes these guys. In some ways they are better friends than he has ever had.

It was a good idea to come up here to Santa Barbara, even if it wasn't Milan's idea in the first place. It really got started with Doctor Seltzer. There was this temporary problem that Milan actually took care of on his own; you know the drill: exercise, vitamins, drop back on the sauce a bit. Stop trying to approach Dale with the notion that he's in any competition with her ex or anyone else for that matter, trying to set records and all that stuff. He and Dale are pretty tight, right? Take it easy. One day at a time. And it isn't as if Dale's giving him any problems. "Don't worry, baby. We've got forty, fifty years ahead of us and then—"

"Yeah?" Milan says. "And then—?"

Dale giggles. "I know about a spa in Mexico where they wean you off all wheat products, sugar, and caffeine." She nudges Milan. "They give you this series of shots and then zowie, instant teenagers."

At first Milan is suspicious. How come Dale is so understanding, all of a sudden, with him having such a problem? Not all that long ago she is telling him how she gets nervous and jumpy if he's reading a new script, getting into rehearsals and two, three days go by and he, uh, he doesn't notice her. And what about that time she visited him on location, waiting in his dressing trailer for him. Milan starts thinking maybe she's so tolerant all of a sudden because she's got something going on the side.

But within a two-month period, Milan finishes a job with a director he never liked, demanding little German sonofabitch: chews sugar-free Gummi bears to keep from smoking, always poking Milan in the sternum with his iPhone and telling him, "Show us what you're really feeling, John. Don't hide it from us." Then in quick succession, Milan fires his agent and gets a new one, a woman with long acrylic nails whom he believes to be an aggressive lesbian.

And suddenly the problem, that's what they've both started calling it, is history, and Dale is making with the jokes. "Well, well. Will you look at who's back in the ballgame? Where've you been hiding it, kiddo?"

Dr. Seltzer is happy for him, but he doesn't let Milan off the hook. "What do you think the problem really was, John?"

The problem was, this director was a real pain and Milan's former agent was a wimp. An aggressive agent can get you an extra hundred, two hundred large and a percentage of gross, none of this net stuff, every time. An aggressive lesbian agent, it's like you've got an annuity.

Should have bailed out on Dr. Seltzer then and there, right? Everything working fine, what do you need them for? But once they get their hooks into you they don't like to let go. That two-fifty an hour adds up, and shrinks have this thing where they believe you aren't getting anywhere—you can't make personal gains, is how they say it—unless you pay them serious rates.

So Milan lets Seltzer talk him into getting away from L.A. Just keep a small condo on Bundy in west L.A. for when he's got meetings or readings. "Think about a rural or semirural setting," Seltzer urges him. When Dale hears this and reacts with such enthusiasm, all Milan's suspicions are gone. If she had something going on the side, last thing she'd want is to leave L.A.

Milan talks it over with some acquaintances, even sets out the situation to Stacy, the new agent. Stacy nods approval. "Santa Barbara," she says. "That has a nice cachet to it." Great word, cachet. He was right to want her as his agent. "And they'll know in advance what it will cost when I tell them, 'I can have John down for a reading in a few hours. He's up in Santa Barbara, you know.'" Milan was thinking of Palm Springs, Rancho Viejo, but Stacy has sold him. It's a good thing she doesn't know how well she's done because, at the moment Milan switches in his mind from Palm Springs to Santa Barbara, he is vulnerable. Stacy could have gotten to him for twenty percent, which some agents are now starting to get.

Milan gets a house from this Santa Barbara real estate guy, Bill Baumgartner? Wears saddle oxfords, ties his hair in a ponytail, and specializes in older estates in Montecito. Milan is feeling pretty good about life when Dr. Seltzer hits him with the capper. "You'd better get a dog, John."

"Pardon me?"

"Rural people tend to mistrust city people as it is. Where you're going, a dog helps." Seltzer taps his teeth with a Mark Cross pen. Dental work must have cost forty, fifty large. "In fact, it should be a very special kind of dog."

"You want me to get a guard dog?"

More physical action from Seltzer than usual. Emphatic head shakes. "What are you trying to hide, John?"

"Don't you ever get tired of that bullshit, Dr. Seltzer?" Shrinks always trying to nail you with symbols and consequences.

Old Seltzer is looking at his two-fifty an hour. "I'm merely trying to examine the possibility that people with guard dogs may have a tendency to overprotectiveness."

Yeah, well Milan has this tendency to off-the-top zingers. He wishes the guys from Xanadu could have been there when he smiles at Seltzer and says, "Okay, you got me cold, Doc. I'm trying to protect my money."

"I'm talking about a dog with a problem, John. A creature you can relate to as we try to enhance your capacity for personal gains."

"I'm back in business with my wife. I've just finished a difficult picture. I've got a very aggressive new agent, and I'm moving to Santa Barbara.," Milan goes. "Spare me personal gains, huh? What could be wrong?"

"Ah," Dr. Seltzer goes, giving a tug at his red vest. Probably wears it to have something to do at moments like this. "That's what we're here to find out." The upshot is, Seltzer sends Milan to this woman, Jean Rickert. She's got a roomful of diplomas, specializes in dogs and cats for people who have, as she puts it, been emotionally short-changed or who are holding back on themselves.

Five minutes with Milan, this Jean Rickert snaps her fingers, writes something on a card, hands it to him. He'll say this for her, she is not a gouge. Less than seventy-five bucks for the session and the recommendation. She knows a dog who is perfect for Milan.

"What's its problem?"

Jean Rickert has a sprinkle of facial freckles and a laughter like a wind chime. "Oh, you'll find out soon enough," she tells him.

So Milan drives to a place in Chatsworth called Animal Friends, pays another hundred bucks, and is given this medium-sized dog, a breed he never heard of before, a Queensland Blue Heeler.

Four, five weeks later, Milan is on the phone to Jean Rickert. "Listen," he says, I've had this dog, Roxie? It's more than a month, and as far as I can see, she's a perfectly normal dog, so what's with her problem?"

When Jean Rickert answers, Milan can visualize her freckles. "You'll find out, John."

— 🐾 —

When Milan, Dale, and Roxie move to Santa Barbara, they see with some frequency graffiti that says "L.A. Go Home." Dr. Seltzer was not only correct in his assessment about how rurals and small-town people tend to resent people from urban areas, but also they seem to resent in particular anyone from Los Angeles—even if they are in the motion picture or television industries. People in Santa Barbara seem to react with more emphasis in either case, and a combination of the two is often seen as deadly.

This is why Milan is so pleased with the way the guys at the Xanadu Coffee Shop accept him. They know who he is, but from the way they treat him, it's as though they didn't. So he doesn't have to be on all the time, carry all the action. Just show up in the morning around eight, eight-fifteen, leave Roxie in the car if it's raining or cold, and otherwise take one of the outside tables. Whoever gets there first gets the table with the best view of the front entrance to Von's of the Stars market. No big deal. Drink coffee, read the paper. Have a cinnamon roll.

These guys are all talented in some way. Milan can sense that from the offhanded way they approach things. Not always looking at how much a thing costs. Never wondering about return on investment or all the things you have to do to keep in the public eye. Not a hint of this new demographics emphasis which, when Milan was first starting out in the business, was always expressed as some money-related question: Will they get it in the Midwest? Will it maybe offend Southerners if a white woman takes an interest in a guy who's dark and didn't get it from a sun tan parlor?

They all came here to get away from always having to be on, calculate effects, call attention to themselves. Maybe that's what binds them, because this is not an easy place to crack. Hasn't been here all that long, but Milan already has a sense of how it goes with all the private clubs along East Valley Road and the members who know perfectly well who you are, but they look right through you and give more time of day to the valets who park their cars.

Milan knows he could make it here on his own; he's always been something of a loner. It's an extra plus, being accepted by these guys, and it's all he can do some mornings to keep from trying to pick up the tab for coffees and rolls. He knows such a gesture would not be cool, would work to his disadvantage. But even if it did, it can't possibly match the disaster that comes down on him now, blind-sides him from the one place he least expected.

— ❧ —

The man asks Milan, "Do you have any idea who I am?" Trim little bastard in pressed khakis, uses a cane. Right in Milan's face at the front door. Milan is about to give him the Mr. Sincerity look, tell him, "I can't quite place the name, but weren't you in the film where you did that brilliant cameo of Hitler?"

Swear to God, the guy's got his hair combed low on his forehead. Small, trimmed moustache. You could make the connection in a minute. But the guy is steaming already, right? No sense adding to the problem, whatever it is, so Milan uses a gambit he picked up from George Bush up at the Bohemian Grove, hasn't missed yet. "I don't believe we've met," he extends his hand. "I'm John Milan."

The man pointedly ignores Milan's offered handshake. "This is not something you can slide over with a little charm, Milan. I happen to be Major Milton Britt, U.S. Marine Corps, retired. It is my responsibility to be head of Neighborhood Watch. I don't suppose that has any significance for you."

Yeah, yeah; it has significance. Milan has heard about the Neighborhood Watch from the guys at the Xanadu, even seen some of their newsletters, *NeighborGram,* can you believe it? A cadre of wealthy retirees. Coupon clippers is more like it. Some of them like this Britt maybe double or triple dipping. Riding around Montecito in unmarked Bentleys, is how the joke goes. Checking on suspicious activities. Making sure the Mexican gardeners don't loaf on the job, maybe slip a cutting out of their patrons' roses for their own gardens or whack off an arm of a cactus, transplant it in their own garden. God forbid the maids at the Miramar or Four Seasons Biltmore score some piece of clothing a guest left behind. Trying to get a law passed English is the official language of the Tri-Counties. Screw the rest of the state. They can do what they want. Keep San Luis Obispo, Santa Barbara, and Ventura Counties English-speaking.

Neighborhood Watch. Give me a break. Act like a vigilante committee, call in at the sheriff's substation to report if things don't look right, such as maybe the carpetbaggers from L.A. having friends who might be professional basketball players, and you know what that means.

But you've got to give Milan credit. He doesn't blink or back up. "Hey, neighbor, why don't you come in for some coffee and we'll see what's on your mind?"

Major Britt shakes his head, giving this ironic take, his you-just-don't-get-it-do-you spin. "I've never been one for those studio tours or gawking at movie stars' homes, Milan. I believe I can come to the point right here." He has a clip board under his arm which he now produces, begins thumbing through papers. "I have the particulars right here."

Particulars? Reminds Milan of the German director.

Britt is gone in five minutes and Milan finds himself in his den, thumbing through his phone book, looking for Jean Rickert's number down in L.A.

"Ah, John," she says when Milan tells him about Major Britt's visit, "I see you finally discovered what Roxie's problem is."

— ?♣ —

"This is a bad business." They're gathered for coffee at the Xanadu Coffee Shop the next morning when Keller looks through the papers Major Britt left with Milan. Shoves the documents to Barnet, who says "Hoo boy," edges them over to Wolfe. "We have to act," Keller says. "Now."

You have to understand, Keller is neither a role model of decisiveness or affability; there are constant digs about his past, his clandestine activities, jibes about him being a National Rifle Association lobbyist, a Contra old boy. So when Wolfe seems to defer, Lessing nods sagely, says, "Didn't I have problems of my own with Molly?" and Burnaby says, "I'm in," a coalition seems to have formed with Keller the acknowledged leader.

"This is just the sort of thing they thrive on," Keller says, out on the table, and before Milan realizes it, he's in that same overdrive buzz landed him in Dr. Seltzer's office in the first place.

"This is only a test, right?" Milan goes. "Had this been a real emergency, you would have been given an emergency warning system number on your radio dial. This is only a test."

Keller shakes his head. "I used to think that, too, when I first came here. Always the test." Now it's this big, significant nod at Milan. "We're a lot more alike than you might think," he goes. "But no, this isn't a test. We're not putting you on. They mean business."

Milan wants to know more about this big similarity with him and Keller, but what he says is "Come on. What can they do?"

"Ah," Keller says. "Everything. They can do everything. They are the established order and tradition, John. Everything they can do, they will."

Queensland Blue Heeler, right? Roxie. A working dog, bred to work the sheep ranches, excuse me, sheep stations in Australia. The way Keller explains it, "Arguably one of the two or three brightest dogs extant, right up there with the Border Collie, who is, of course, number one, and some of your Australian shepherds. Pound-for-pound, optimal delivery." No wonder Keller gives Milan the creeps, makes everything sound like a goddamn weapon.

So part of the Queensland Blue Heeler apparatus package—swear to God, he actually called it that—is the tendency to nip its quarry if the quarry doesn't respond immediately.

"You mean bite?" Milan says.

"Well, yes. You could call it that, which is the crux of the problem. The dog is not biting out of meanness or conviction, as in say, your Rottweiler, or your Doberman pinscher guard dog. They take no pleasure in breaking skin or shredding flesh. The nipping is merely an instinct, a well-designed trait, if you will, a functional device to deliver cows or sheep from point A to point B, a task at which the dog excels."

"Then it's his nature, for chrissake," Milan says, aware now that Wolfe is giving him this strange look. "What?" he goes.

"Salinger, isn't it?" Wolfe seems to be musing. "*The Catcher in the Rye.* Nothing like subtext, is there, John?"

Brits. You never know what they're thinking. Always out there on some kind of edge, like we get Elvis sightings, the Brits probably have Winston Churchill sightings. The glory that was. You know? "Dog never bit—nipped—me," he goes. "Sweet as pie with Dale. Has she ever nipped any of you guys?"

"We are not quarry," Barnet says.

Sadly, Keller agrees. "We are not, but somehow Milton Britt, U.S.M.C., retired, is."

Roxie has not only bitten Major Britt, but also she has compounded the legal doctrine of "scienter," in which a dog is given the moral equivalent of one free bite; Roxie went back for seconds and broke the skin.

Maybe there is some encyclopedia known to every career military person, listing poisons, muzzle velocities, amounts of powder needed to blow up people or things. Perhaps Major Britt has not only therein documented the nipping proclivities indigenous to the Blue Heeler, but also he's even got that nice kid, Craig, down at Montecito Pet Shop, on tape, saying, "A great breed for the right person, but they are known to be nippers." No help from the fact that Craig is not a fan of Major Britt or the Neighborhood Watch. "Oh, wow," Craig says later on, "you mean that asshole is going to quote me on this?" Cold comfort that Craig is, as they say, a hostile witness.

"Now," Keller says. "We have to move right now."

"Well, excuse me," Milan says. "I'll go right over and get some black shoe polish for my face."

Keller looks at the documents. "He means to have the dog destroyed as an example."

"I'll fight," Milan says. "I can afford Dr. Seltzer, I guess I can afford Dershowitz, F. Lee Bailey."

"You don't have time," Keller says. "Once that dog is in quarantine, there could easily be an accident."

"I've got a place," Burnaby says.

Keller nods.

"What?" Milan says.

"You can't know," Keller says. "You have to be out of the loop. When they question you, and they will, it is essential you not know anything."

"Don't be a *creep*," Milan tells him.

"I know how it sounds," Keller says. "Say good-bye. Tell her to trust us."

"I don't believe this," Milan says.

"Put the leash on her," Burnaby goes. "Let her see you doing it. Give her a pat, then hand the leash to Keller."

"This is—this is not real," Milan says.

"This is very real," Keller says.

Ten minutes later, he is alone at the table facing the Von's of the Stars, peripherally aware of at least two twos and a three, entering to do their morning shopping, wishing he could point them out to Wolfe and Barnet.

The next morning he is first there to nail down the table. The more he thinks of it, the more he is convinced now they are putting him on, and indeed, last night he even told Dale he'd like to have a little barbecue or something at the house, invite some of his coffee friends over, celebrate his birthday coming up. But after they all show up, business as usual, and a half hour elapses, not one mention of Roxie, Milan chokes up. This is not that Robert DeNiro restraint where, you know, DeNiro looks like he's trying not to cry to make you see how touched he is. Milan is into it, using moves the German director never saw.

"I just want to say I'm touched you guys would do this for me."

"You'd better leave it alone," Keller says.

"No," Wolfe goes. "Let him hear it."

Keller defers to Wolfe.

"I'll do it," Barnet says. He embraces Milan. "John, we didn't do it for you."

"Excuse me?"

"Roxie is a remarkable dog."

"Wait a minute. What you're saying is—what you guys mean is—"

"He's got it," Wolfe says. "I think he's got it."

Dale comes over to sit on the arm of his overstuffed leather den chair and tousle his hair. "You know, Sweetie," she says, "I've been thinking. You'd look good with a moustache. A big, bushy one."

The fuck kind of thing is that to tell a man on his fiftieth birthday? He is sitting here nursing a Glenlivet; please note it is his only one of the day so far, trying to resist the temptation to get bagged, trying to get into the mood to take Dale out to dinner, celebrate a little, or call in some friends. The enormity of being a full half-century he can handle, if that were all there was to it. But Milan misses Roxie, feels somehow diminished without her. You add to that the people he thought were doing this truly great thing for him, and now his wife wants a moustache. That calls attention away from what? A weak mouth?

"I miss that goddamn dog," he tells Jean Rickert on a phone call. "Ah, John," she tells him. "That is her redemptive power."

"You wouldn't be English by any chance?"

"Rickert is a fine Scots name, John."

Later in the day, Dale comes in, asks if he wants her to call in some people from L.A., maybe his agent, some friends, have Pierre La Fond send over a catered buffet. Maybe the guys from Xanadu.

"They'd come if Roxie were here," Milan agonizes.

"Oh, Sweetie," Dale says. "It isn't so bad." She offers to build him another Glenlivet, he says screw it, opts for coffee. When she comes in with the tray, Dale also has the phone.

Milan is suspicious because of all the calls from the sheriff's department, the animal shelter, and this Notice to Show Cause, and to produce that certain canine known as Roxie or face contempt proceedings from the Municipal Court of Santa Barbara County. "I'm telling you," he says into the phone, "I don't have the animal. I don't know where she is."

"It's Keller, John. I know what today is."

So you called to sing "Happy Birthday," right? He's close, but he doesn't say it. He waits Keller out.

"Do you know where the Cold Springs School is, John?"

"Up on East Valley?"

"Near the fire station. You might want to be there at sunset."

"What do you mean?"

"Happy Birthday, John." The line goes dead.

— ❧ —

The playground of the Cold Springs School seems surreal in the long shadows as Milan starts toward the swings. A few raucous crows chatter in the sycamores. A horned owl offers footnote commentary over the rustle of leaves in the evening rush of cool air down from the mountains.

"Half a century and what to show for it but possessions?" Milan asks himself.

There is movement in a stand of trees just beyond the kindergarten playground. Milan advances toward it. Although there is still some light, the figure he sees is indistinct.

A voice projects out on the moist evening. "Fifteen minutes, Milan."

This time, Milan loses it, goes over the top. "Synchronize your watches, right?"

But then he notes a small, compact form approaching him, and he does not hesitate in his rush to meet it.

Death Watches

Richard Martin's death took place on a weekend where there was no climatic disaster or impending military clash anywhere in the world. No rock star had been a suicide, no professional athlete had battered a woman, and no politician was facing public outrage for soliciting sexual favors. It was almost, Ben Langer decided, as though Martin had picked this crisp, sweet weekend in early April on purpose, crashing his light plane on an island off the coast of Maine while on an idiosyncratic flight plan to the opening of his new exhibition in Montreal as a means of giving his work yet another boost up the escarpment of public esteem.

A representative from Martin's family immediately contacted Langer, requesting him to do the valedictory. "I'm pleased to speak about him in public," Langer told the distant cousin, who now stood to inherit big time, "but I hope your choice of me has nothing to do with the prediction."

The distant cousin spoke with the smugness of someone who already knew the contents of Martin's will. "This has nothing to do with your prediction," he said. "I'm asking you," he said, "because Richard considered you a friend and had great respect for some of the unpopular choices you've made in your own life."

At once chastened and relieved, Langer set to work composing a eulogy suitable for someone as complex and difficult to reckon as Martin had been. Of all the friends, former students, and hangers-on in the group, Richard Martin, still in his mid-fifties, had been Langer's candidate for an early and dramatic death. This was as well known as Langer's assertion that Breckenridge, the transplanted poet from Texas, would outlive them all; that Barnet would be the first in their midst to win a Pulitzer Prize; and that Lilly Fell would be the first among them to be short-listed for the National Book Award.

These observations make Langer seem given to judgmental pronouncements about his friends and colleagues. In reality, Langer was a private man. He often feared in secret that the standards to which he held himself were suffering from anemia. The discovery he dreaded most in his biannual medical check-ups was not an alarming serum cholesterol level such as the one that still caused Lefkowitz to tremble at the sight of an egg; not a network of clogged arteries like those discovered in the chest of Binford; not even prostate hypertrophy, however benign, that cost Dugan any sense of spontaneity in his sex life. Langer feared the moment when Dr. Rodgers would rummage through the pockets of his smock, then withdraw a Reese's Peanut Butter Cup for each of them, and lay the prognosis on the line.

"Ben, we seem to have a problem with a missing gene."

"Just tell me this, Stan. Is there something we can take for it?"

"Sarcasm won't do it, Ben. You're simply going to have to learn to live with having fewer opinions than most people."

Hyperbole, of course, but even with the humor of exaggeration, Langer felt in a constant state of being one-down. As if to compensate himself for his lack of opinions, he had visions of people, many of whom were so wild or farcical in nature as to endear him to individuals he did not like. On the other hand, Langer had been right about Barnet's Pulitzer, and Lilly Fell's recent books did carry a banner proclaiming her a winner of the National Book Award.

Now, they were rushing Martin's body back to California, no doubt too late to inter his remains within twenty-four hours of his death, but close enough to acknowledge the man's relationship with a religion he treated with the roughness and tenderness of the slabs of stone he gouged, chiseled at, and drew rasps over with those big, expressive hands of his.

While Langer set down on paper the impressions about Martin he would read at the service, it came to him as heavy irony that Martin, so often convivial, wanting to make room for others at the table, had died alone. So, too, had Feldman, that wry, deadpan storyteller whose affectation of dark suits had earned him the nickname of "The Undertaker."

And Gallarza, breathing his last all by himself, while his family argued in the hospital waiting room about the morality of taking him off life supports. Langer's recollection of Gallarza's death-watch companion was an "I Love Lucy" rerun with the volume turned off.

Langer had been privy to the most outrageous cosmic joke of all when he'd traveled to American Samoa to bring back the remains of Diarmuid Phillips. The legendary Irish writer had been lent a house there by a grateful fan. There, it was supposed, he could finish his big novel, *Along the River Run,* having a tidy advance on royalties and no distractions, notably none of his ex-wives. There was also a burly servant with strict instructions about the spindly Phillips's wine rations. On a spree to celebrate completion of the work, Phillips had a heart attack. His life trailed away in the company of the servant, whose command of English was limited to a phrase book for American servicemen during World War II.

Langer shuddered every time he thought of it: Phillips urging a book of Yeats on the servant. "Read to me, man. Anything from this book. If I'm to die, at least I can have the sound of angels in my ears."

"Can you direct me to a good restaurant?"

"Aw, God, man! Can't you see I'm dying?"

"Some afternoons, the rains come early."

— 🕭 —

Moved by his own eloquence about Richard Martin as a communicator of human passions, Langer grew damp-eyed watching friends, students, acquaintances, and distant relatives who were scheduled to inherit, file past the grave site, where they would toss a parting handful of dirt onto Martin's coffin. He heard Maggie Meeker whisper, "You're not alone any more, Richard," when she tossed her handful of dirt and a flower she had somehow filched from a display.

Allegra Neal tossed a nosegay along with her handful of dirt. "Adios," she said. Langer was so moved by these ritual gestures that he mourned not only Richard Martin, but also all those he knew who had been unfortunate enough to die alone. What an unspeakable tragedy it seemed, a travesty on the well-lived life. "Even the attempted well-lived life," he muttered to himself when it became his turn to toss a handful of dust onto Richard Martin's coffin.

These moments built a sturdy resolve within Langer. The best way to commemorate Martin's death was to do everything within his power to avoid a solitary death for himself.

— ❧ —

Langer poured a healthy splash of cognac into his coffee before dialing the telephone number of Allegra Neal. The sight of her at the funeral had filled him with the conflicting emotions of a man who'd allowed a trivial flirtation to come between his sincere passion for Allegra and his embarkation on an erotic vacation.

In her late forties, slightly more Reubenesque than when they'd lived together, Allegra radiated a musky intelligence and anima under her stylish mourning blacks. Yet even more apparent to Langer was the tacit awareness and stature of the teacher-writer whose arcane specialty, the pre-Raphaelites, brought standing-room-only audiences to her classes, a full-page review of her latest book in *Rolling Stone,* and the grudging approval of an academic community that considered reviews in *Rolling Stone*, however fulsome, beneath academic standards of dignity.

Langer recalled Wolfe, shaking his head in respectful wonderment of Allegra's accomplishment. "The Pre-Raphaelites, for

God's sake! I mean, can you imagine if she'd taken on something huge like *The Fairy-Queen*?

The complexity here for Langer was that Allegra, brought by circumstances to being unattached again, would think Langer was trying to fan old sparks, hopeful of warming his ardor, so to speak, in the bed he had forsaken with such cavalier brio. How to make her see the larger issue? He topped off his coffee with yet more cognac, sipped, and dialed.

Allegra picked up on the first ring, and before Langer would get in a word, confronted him. "Is that you, Ben?"

Langer sputtered. "How could you possibly know it was me? We haven't talked in a year."

'Two years."

"How could you know it was me?"

"Who else do I know who calls right after the rates change?"

"We're in the same city, goddamnit. This has nothing to do with rates."

"Old habits die hard, Ben. Whenever you were away, even if it was only to L.A., you'd always wait for the evening rates."

"Are you implying I'm cheap? Is that what this is about?"

"You always have an agenda, Ben. You always want something. *That's* what this is about. I find it very convenient you should call within two weeks of my getting a teaching assistant who just happens to fit your libido profile."

Langer loosed a bark of frustration. "What libido profile? I don't have a libido profile."

"Right. Of course," Allegra snickered. "What about cheerleader type? Blonde hair. Preternaturally bright. Young, Ben. Notably young. A tattoo somewhere. Ankle or shoulder, probably. That libido type. Like, say, Tansy Patton."

"A man makes one mistake, one lousy mistake and suddenly it's a libido type. Where's the epistemology in a judgment like that?"

"Just behind your zipper, Ben. And no, I will not give you her phone number."

"I don't want her number. I didn't even know you had a new

assistant. I don't want anyone's number. In point of fact, Allegra, all I want is a rather special favor."

Her laughter infuriated him. "What's so damn funny?"

"It's like—" she laughed again and Langer felt his bile churn.

"It's like what?"

"It's like you used to ask for oral sex. How many times do I have to tell you? You don't ask for oral sex. You get it. You give it. But you don't ask."

"I'm not talking about oral sex. What I'm trying to talk about is—"

"You want something back. It has to be you want something back. Those god-awful onyx bookends you bought in Mexico."

"I don't want the bookends, Allegra. What I want is—Ah, God! Martin is dead and what I want is to make sure—"

"You've got a lot of nerve, mister. Calling to ask if he and I had anything going. You gave up any privilege to know when you went off with Tansy. If that's what's itching your curiosity, mister, then you can just itch away."

By then, Langer was recalling some of the arguments that were so much a part of their relationship. In time he'd grown to think of them as condiments for the Allegra-Ben bouillabaisse. "I'll tell you what's itching me," he said. "I'll tell you. Of all the people I could ask, what could have possessed me to think of asking you?"

"Old habits, Ben." And the line went dead.

— ❧ —

Langer arrived at the Xanadu Coffee Shop shortly after eight-thirty, ordered his coffee, selected a sticky bun, and joined the others at the large table in the courtyard. Barnet and Halevy scooted chairs to make room for him. But before Langer could exchange greetings, his arrival was overshadowed by Maggie Meeker, his reason for being out this morning in the first place, reaching a dramatic moment in her narrative. "And then," Maggie sputtered, "and then, in the very midst of an act of serious intimacy, the son of a bitch stopped what we were doing and he committed this—this unspeakable insensitivity."

"And that," Wolfe, ever the director, prompted, "is when you decided to dump him?"

Maggie nodded in emphasis, her coils of frizzed, sun-bleached hair bouncing agreement. "From that moment, he was toast." She paused for a sip of her cappuccino. "We didn't even bother to finish what we were doing. It was over, right then."

Langer soon had the impression that Maggie was silently polling the audience for their nods of understanding, but even more to the point, their sympathy. "I've been good about his calling me Mag-Mag during moments of passion," she continued. "After all, how could he know that was the name my father called me to get my goat? I've been patient with his snoring, and I even went along with that wild-ass scheme of his for converting the spare bedroom into a hydroponics garden."

Maggie's glazed expression reminded Langer of the expressions on the faces of recent survivors of mud slides, earthquakes, or summer fires. "You sleep with someone and share meals with him," she said, "you fight over things like two-percent milk or fat free, you argue about preferences in brand names at the drugstore, and all the while you think you know him."

Langer had for some time regretted that there appeared to be no real chemistry or intimacy between him and Maggie Meeker. Over the long years of their friendship, her energy levels, her dramatic intensity, and her eclectic brightness appealed to him. True, she was a bit daft and conflicted, causing him to observe once that she embodied the qualities of all of Lear's daughters in one convenient package. He had even referred to her in conversation as time-release angst, but this was not meant in ridicule. Maggie's spiky, reflexive nature seemed to Langer to be a perfect complement to his own more reflective landscape, and her message on his answering tape, urging him to be present this morning, had left him feeling upbeat. So what if she had a boyfriend? No one in the group took this man, Gunther, seriously. His most visible talent was his ability to tune Mercedes-

Benzes. Where was the value or, for that matter, longevity in a thing like that?

Maggie looked up from her reverie, drank some coffee, and made eye contact across the table with Langer. "Thank you for coming, Ben. I wanted you to hear this."

Halevy nudged him under the table. For no reason he could identify, Langer felt his heart lighten, his innards fizz. After his dismal encounter with Allegra, he had been deflated, wondering if his concern about being alone when he died was simply a large flock of karmic pigeons coming home to roost. Perhaps a lonely death was to be his reward for a life spent reading or listening to music or the solitary ramblings needed to bring him to terms with the times when he had to be with people.

"What," he asked Barnet, "was this heinous crime of Gunther's that she should banish him? Another woman?"

"Funny you should ask," Barnet said sotto voce. "While they were in flagrante, as it were, Gunther used the L-word."

"Excuse me?"

"Gunther told Miss Maggie," Barnet said, then chortled into his coffee, "that he loved her."

— 🙢 —

"Can you imagine a person saying such a thing, and at such a time?"

Although there was a hint of a question in Maggie Meeker's delivery, Langer was more aware of a sense of outrage, sputtering through the coils of her being, like steam in the radiator of a cheap hotel room. They were now some blocks away from the Xanadu Coffee Shop, moved to a new coffee shop, The Coffee Bean, on lower Coast Village Road where they hoped to talk with less danger of interruption. On the walls about them, a nod to local artists, were framed drawings of cavorting horses.

"As a matter of fact," Langer ventured with some deliberation, "I can."

Maggie Meeker loved audiences, a favor that was generally returned not only because she was attractive in a freckled, bony

100

way, but also as a consequence of bracelets, necklaces, earrings, and belts she wore that tended to clank. Langer was also taken with her posture, her husky contralto diction, and things she did with her hands that suggested an ongoing game of cat's cradle.

"I can see," Langer edged forth his thesis, "a very definite reason for saying such a thing at such a time." This was beginning to be heady stuff for Langer, as it came to him with sudden aching clarity that Maggie had an agenda for bringing him here, away from the greater possibility that they would be noticed and insinuated upon by some acquaintance. Without Gunther in her life, she'd be on the prowl. Maggie did not tend to remain alone for long. Gunther's predecessor had lasted nearly five years before Maggie's announcement that he was toast. Although one robin hardly indicated a Spring, Langer began now to sense a pattern. Before Gunther had been—Roger? Yes; Roger, the New Age astrologer. And before him, before the lexicon of toast had been extended to mean finite, terminal, done, extinct, there had been Ned, a securities analyst.

What in common would a securities analyst, a New Age astrologer, and a board-certified Mercedes-Benz mechanic have? But in the very depths of his now fluttering heart, Langer knew. They had all come to believe they loved Maggie, hadn't they?

"That's why I called you," she told Langer. "You are in many ways the voice of reason."

Langer had made to reach for his cruller, but Maggie, misinterpreting, took the gesture to mean something else. She reached out to claim his hand, enclosing it in both hers and squeezing. "Dear Ben," she said. "How long have we known one another?"

Langer was already wondering how many of his bookcases he could do without, assigning them to her. If she had as much clothing as he thought she did, he could let her have most of the master bedroom and move his fall and winter things to the guest room.

'Tell me I did the right thing, getting rid of Gunther."

Langer considered his own interests in the potential matter. His gaze was drawn to one of the stylized drawings of a horse, its back seeming to be more contorted than a horse could stand. He spoke with deliberation. "If you have to ask, you already know."

He turned away from the horse, mentally thanking it for causing him to look at its uneasy posture. When he tried to free his hand, Maggie tugged at it. "I knew I could rely on you. Now tell me, dear friend, my voice of rational clarity. What reason could a man have for saying such a thing as he did at such a time?" Her face was a freckled map of encouragement. "This is positively Kierkegaardian."

Langer finally got his hand back. "It isn't like Kierkegaardian at all. I believe it would be quite appropriate to say something of that sort during an intimate moment if you were genuinely moved and wanted to forge something—something long lasting with a partner."

"What about *carpe diem,* Ben? What about simply living in the moment? What about the delicious essence of freedom?"

"Genuine fondness can be in the moment *and* over the long haul."

"Romantic twaddle," Maggie sneered. "You're not answering with your mind, Ben." Her brow puckered. "You, of all people. You'd never say a thing like that under those circumstances. Tell me the truth." Appearing to sense that she was on the right track, Maggie bored in, her face close to his. Langer could feel the sparks gaping and crackling between them, even if she could not. "Have you ever, in your mature life—adolescence doesn't count, because they'll say anything—have you ever told that to another person while making love?"

Langer sighed against his will. "No," he said.

"There! I knew it. Not Ben. Not you."

Langer felt his insides begin to churn. "What, not me? Why not? Why wouldn't I say such a thing?"

"Because," Maggie said, "you simply aren't the type. And if you come home with me now, I'll prove it to you."

"Thank you for the kindness of the offer," Langer said. "But I have a desk filled with things that need doing. Swindell has already called twice for a review I owe him, and the animal shelter is holding a cat for my inspection. Besides," he said, gathering his courage, "I'm afraid I might disappoint you." He caught sight of the unfortunate horse for a moment. "This has nothing to do with performance, you understand. It is—it has become a matter of principle."

Reaching his car, Langer continued to feel agitated to the point where he could not yet countenance going home. The matter of principle he'd proclaimed to Maggie Meeker seemed somehow tied not only to the speculative truth but also to an absolute truth as well. The desk filled with things to be looked at and replaced was no abstraction; by any standards Langer had things to do. The review for Swindell was not only no abstraction, but also it was a moral problem as well. What did a man who had been shorted on opinions say about a book he did not really appreciate?

The cat at the animal shelter was another matter. There was no such cat. Langer in fact had no idea where the notion of a cat had come from. But now, having used a cat at the animal shelter as a part of the landscape of his moral high ground in confronting Maggie, Langer felt obliged to visit the animal shelter, look at cats, and give serious consideration to bringing one home.

He drove toward the animal shelter on Overpass Road, allowing the idea of a cat in his life to sink in. By the time he pulled off the Freeway and on to Patterson, the idea seemed not to be all that strange. It might even be comforting to have another living being prowling and fussing among his books, papers, and record collection. Someone with ears to scratch. Someone to share tidbits of liver. Someone to pounce on Langer's bed at four in the morning, kneading and purring on the bedclothes.

For a time, the animal shelter reminded him of visiting friends in the hospital. There was an all-pervading scent of some solvent that all institutions sprayed about to make the surroundings seem clean and efficient, whether they were or not. Men with ponytails wrapped in rubber bands strode with purpose, wearing Rockport brogans that sounded on the waxed floors like suppressed giggles. Volunteer women, who appeared as though they would burst into tears over the slightest hitch in the universe, hovered over counters, chewing on pencils, and neatening stacks of fliers heralding the virtues of neutering or spaying cats.

Langer was led into a corridor of wall-to-ceiling cat cages by an earnest young woman with a tattoo of her astrological sign (Proud to be an Aries) on her shoulder. He decided he would look for a suitable male, whom he would name Abelard. But in the course of his peering into cages and being alternately hissed at or ignored, he came upon a splotched tricolor whose air of total confidence won him over. When he reached into the cage, the cat butted her head against his hand. "Very well," he told the cat, "you shall be Heloise."

But when Langer returned to the main office to claim his prize, he was served by a woman who wore a turtleneck sweater and tied her straw-colored hair into a severe bun. He put the paperwork in front of the woman. "I'm claiming cat number thirty-four."

The woman's name tag, also supporting the imperative to spay or neuter cats, designated her as Claudia. She studied him for a long, critical moment. "I'm very sorry," Claudia said, "I can't let you take her."

In the moments since Langer had made his choice of Heloise, he'd already come to have proprietary feelings about her. "There was no sign on the cage indicating she'd been spoken for."

"She hasn't been." Claudia splayed both hands on the counter. "I simply can't let *you* take her."

"This is a place that puts cats up for adoption," Langer said. "I have found a cat I very much fancy. I wish to adopt her."

Claudia shook her head. "My sorrow is genuine."

Langer felt himself grow cautious. "I think we've managed to get off on the wrong foot somehow," he ventured. "I hope to adopt cat number thirty-four. I'll give her a good home, take good care of her, make sure she gets all her shots."

Claudia plucked the registration card from Langer and scanned it. "She's had her shots."

"Then I'm afraid I don't understand. Why can't I have this cat?"

Claudia consulted the form again. "Mr. Langer, is it?" She paused to allow Langer to ratify himself with a nod. "I can't let you have this cat, Mr. Langer, because you aren't a cat person."

"Excuse me?"

"You don't relate well to cats."

"I came here for the express purpose of adopting a cat. I find one to my liking and propose to take it home, yet you stand there and tell me I don't relate to cats? This is not rational."

Claudia's eyes met his with an incandescent surge. "I know, Mr. Langer. Not being a cat person isn't a rational thing."

"How can you—" Langer became aware of people in the office beginning to look at him. He lowered his voice. "How can you make such a snap judgment? You hardly know me." Langer felt his passion rise. He no longer cared if he was speaking in a loud voice. "Look, I want that cat. You have no right to withhold that cat."

Claudia offered him a sweet smile. "You're probably a very nice man, Mr. Langer. I'm sure you contribute more than your share to society. You undoubtedly have friends who think the world of you, and a family who—"

"I don't have a family," Langer said. "Why do you think I want a cat?"

"I'm sorry for your plight, Mr. Langer," Claudia said. "I truly am. But if it's any comfort to you, some people just aren't cat people, and you happen to be one of them."

"If it's any comfort to you, I am not a mister, I am a professor, and you are not my only recourse. There's more than one way—"

"There!" Claudia said. "I was right. All along, I was right."

Ninety minutes later, Langer was back on Coast Village Road at the pet store, not too far from where he'd started that morning at the coffee klatch. True, he'd stopped in at the small bar off the dining room at Tre Lune for an espresso and a cognac. True, he'd stayed on for a second while delivering a blistering diatribe on bureaucracy, but when he saw that his railings were only bewildering the bartender, he did not even ask, as he was tempted to do, if he looked like a cat person, or if the bartender thought there were people who could tell one way or another.

At the Montecito Pet Shop he strolled about the store, studying large bags of kibble, reading the setup instructions on fish tanks, and browsing the display cards of the various types of identification medallions for cats. After some time he approached Craig, the manager, reminding him of the times he'd bought kibble and chew toys there for Allegra's animals, then with studied indifference, wondering if Craig had any interesting kittens on the premises for sale.

"Couple of real neat short hairs, Mr. Langer. Nice, sturdy domestics with orangey coats. Marmalades. But—"

"But?" Langer said. "But what?"

Craig studied him for a long moment. "Are you sure you wouldn't be happier with a puppy?"

— 🐾 —

The sauce began to curdle for the second time, taking the appearance of menacing ooze from a cheap science fiction film of the '60s. This had a dismaying effect on Langer because he was nearly out of butter. Trying the time-honored method of folding in a beaten egg to coax the sauce's destiny in the right direction, Langer only succeeded in scorching the bottom of a skillet.

Sauce was not an absolute requisite; but his plans for dinner did not allow for substitutions or reckless, eat-over-the-sink strategies he often employed when cooking for himself. This meal was to be what Langer called a sanity dinner, prepared from scratch, served on good china, accompanied by splendid wine, eaten at leisure. None of the ramen cups from Trader Joe's, where one added boiling water, waited for seven minutes, and then plunged in with a stainless steel fork. No frozen vegetables. No bottled sauces, which covered a multitude of sins yet precluded any sense of taste. Not even the canned pates, exotic nut butters in whimsical containers, or jars of pesto made with every kind of green vegetable except basil, all of which seemed to come Langer's way every year around Christmas or Easter.

For Langer, a sanity dinner was a ritual to be indulged at times of greatest need, when things got out of hand, when the pleasure in the small routines of learning and observation were threatened by the universe, advancing with muddy shoes over the carpeting of individual satisfaction. If the sauce could not be uncurdled, Langer's ace-in-the hole was to be fresh mayonnaise, made from fresh eggs and a fruity olive oil. It had worked well in the past, and it would go with the fresh asparagus he'd found at the farmer's market, the osso buco already at roast in the oven, and the Buttonwood pinot noir, at this very moment opened to breathe. With such a meal, Langer would not have to resort to more than one bottle of wine and the more-or-less planned counterirritant factor of a hangover.

Taking out the eggs and oil for the mayonnaise, Langer began to feel like a man in charge. To be sure, he was a man beset. Things were not going his way, but the roasting marrow bones for the osso buco sent an earthy aroma into his dining area, the Buttonwood pinot noir glinted invitation in the fading afternoon, and the organic asparagus lay on the kitchen counter like an Oriental flower display.

Langer flinched but did not falter from his optimism when the front doorbell rang. He moved to the door with crane-like steps, avoiding piles of books, stacks of unread scholarly journals, and a spread of plastic compact disc containers.

A bearded man with acne-pitted cheeks and rheumy eyes that shifted about the interior of Langer's living room as though searching for a weapons cache stood next to a plump, motherly woman dressed in a gray uniform that could have been the habit of a religious order or the issue of some institution. "We've come," the man said, making eye contact with Langer, "for your signature." He thrust forth a clipboard, a sheaf of rumpled papers pinned to its base. "All of your neighbors have signed," he said in summary judgment.

"Some," the woman said, "have even given modest contributions."

The bearded man seemed pained by this, but he extended the clip- board once again.

Langer lived in the part of town variously referred to as Lower East or Baja Riviera. He was used to petitions, funding for Little League teams named for Che Guevara or Caesar Chavez. He had, somewhere, a drawer filled with pyramidal wedges of chocolate being sold for charitable purposes. There were occasional inquiries about the state of his soul, his preparedness for Armageddon, and requests from consortiums of ethnic gardeners to help repeal anti-leaf-blowing ordinances.

"You, of all people, should sympathize with this," the bearded man said. Yet again the clipboard was thrust.

Langer, seized with impatience, wrested the clipboard from the man, scribbled his name on one of the available lines of the petition, and shut the door without bothering to ask about the cause or the nature of the advocacy at work here.

Halfway back to the kitchen, he was visited by a contrary feeling, a sense that he had been mean-spirited. Mean-spirited people deserved to die alone. Perhaps that was even the common thread among all those who did die with neither friends nor family in attendance.

He turned to the door, determined to give this unappetizing pair some part of his attention and quite possibly a tithe from his wallet. In any case, he was willing to listen. But when he opened the door, he found instead Allegra Neal, flanked by two large shopping bags from Trader Joe's, poised to knock.

Ever since Langer had known Allegra, people were saying of her that the passing years had been kind to her. The impression was strong with him now as he realized she was doing nothing to conceal the gray that had long ago begun to insinuate its way into her thick mane of reddish brown hair. Indeed, she even seemed to be welcoming the presence of gray by allowing a full growth to swirl about her elongated oval of a face.

"You're staring," Allegra said.

"What is it, two, three years since we've seen each other?

And it's like we've kept an argument going. I was staring because I wasn't expecting you, and you used to be more vain about the color of your hair."

"Not *an* argument, Ben. *The* argument." She reached for the string handles of the shopping bags and in the process of her lifting, Langer could see that they bore heavy contents. "And by the way, I'm still vain about it."

He made an elaborate gesture of inviting her inside, which she accepted by moving past him and into the living room, taking in the furnishings, the sources of light, possibly even inspecting for traces of cobwebs and dust bunnies. He was immediately furious.

"It came to me that I may have been harsh with you when we talked the other day," she said. "I'm not a mean-spirited person—except with you."

"I'm not going to touch that," Langer said. "Will you take some wine?"

"Yes, please." She set the shopping bags on top of an end table next to a flowery chintz-covered sofa. "Early American thrift shop?" she hitched her head toward the sofa. "There I go again. I'm sorry. I had no call to say that. It's really a nice sofa." She lowered herself onto it, waiting for him to pour her a glass of the pinot noir.

"I came here," she said, "to bring you some of your things back. There's no reason why you shouldn't have those book ends. There's that fake Tiffany lamp you liked so much and some candle holders."

"Dammit, Allegra, I don't want the book ends. I bought them for you. And I never cared all that much for candles. You're the one who likes candles."

"I remember clearly you said the bookends were for us. For *our* things. Not for my things. Not for your things." She made a waving gesture with both hands, as though cooling soup, as though making words go away. Nothing seemed to help. She sipped wine, smacked her lips, and looked more closely at the glass.

Langer caught himself being defensive. "That's a good wine."

"I know," Allegra said. "It's not like you to serve such wine unless—" Then she sniffed. "That's osso buco. You're preparing a seduction dinner."

"I'm not expecting anyone."

"Oh, right. Of course." Allegra stood. "I'll just leave these things and be on my way. This must be terribly awkward for you and I must say, you're being a gentleman about it."

"I am not expecting anyone."

"You don't have to cover your tracks, Ben. I'd simply like to be out of here before I have to see her."

"There isn't any her, I'm telling you. I wish—I wish there were." Langer was frequently surprised when the theatrical parts of him got loose like this and wanted a larger role to play. He reached for the glass of wine, handed it to her, and lowered his voice to a more conversational tone. "For the love of God, woman, do we have to do this to each other?"

Allegra took a sip of the wine and blinked her hooded eyes. "Yes," she said, "I guess we do."

When she was gone Langer sipped from the wine remaining in what had been Allegra's glass. The darkness of the evening pressed in and the sounds of the neighborhood began to emerge. A dog barked. Someone yelled at it to shut up. A baby cried. Someone yelled for someone else to change it. A boom box sounded. Someone yelled for someone else to turn up the volume. Canned laughter from two different television comedies flared up in a brief territorial squabble.

Langer sat in the emerging night for a time trying to map the source of his grief. The sadness this time had begun with the news of Richard Martin's death. Then, the sadness had begun to spread, like a spilled glass of wine on someone's table cloth, taking up friendships, loves, old relationships, future possibilities, and, of course Langer's own sense of his own longevity.

He rummaged through the shopping bags left by Allegra until he found a candlestick with a good-sized stub of remaining candle. The discovery cheered him. No sense mourning alone. He needed to use his pocket knife to cut the candle stub in two, then expose enough wick to light each piece. He watched them burn until he was sure they'd had caught and then he returned to the kitchen.

Love Will Make You Drink and Gamble, Stay Out Late at Night

> "......a world ful tikel......"
> — Geoffrey Chaucer, *The Miller's Tale*

While he waits for the bartender at Tom & Jerry's to take his order, Jack Carter notices the man in the tuxedo, bow-tie flopped open, sitting two stools away, sipping a frothy amber liquid from a tall glass. "Newcastle," comes the reply to Carter's inquisitive glance. "Newcastle Ale on tap."

Carter was ordering Perrier water or San Pellegrino when he started the evening. He switched at The Intermezzo, because it would have been silly not to have at least a glass of one of their pinot noirs. There was a fair merlot at the San Ysidro Ranch and, surprise, the Biltmore had a fantastic new zinfandel from Foxen.

Carter is no ale or beer drinker, not like David Burns, whom he's trying to educate to the finer side of the local varietal wines. But Carter is feeling reckless now, primed for the adventure he has planned, and what are the chances Tom & Jerry's would have anything but plonk? So what the hell; "Newcastle," he tells the bartender. "Newcastle it is, then."

He has no illusions about the Newcastle being any less potent than what he's been drinking, but at least the effect will be spread out over a greater volume, giving him more time and a greater chance for things to work as planned.

After a few sips, he nods his approval at the man in the tux. In a matter of minutes, he has that sense of flying, the thrill of anticipation and confidence that warn him: This glass of ale represents the crucial balance. He needs to nurse it if he is to have any hope of being able to drive, should it become necessary for him to try another place.

"No need to worry, man. Live it up," the man at the bar says. "Big motel, right around the corner. Many's the night—" He rolls his eyes.

Carter knows all about the motel. The motel was one of the reasons he'd come here in the first place. There was a motel near The Intermezzo. Plenty of room possibilities at the Ranch or the Biltmore.

"I drive all the way across town for the Newcastle," the man in the tux ventures.

"Eighty, ninety dollars for a motel is a small price to pay when you compare it to the cost of a DUI." He tilts his glass to Carter in affable salute. "I amortize the glasses of ale I drink against the price of the motel room. Two, three bucks a glass is nothing compared to what they'd fine you if you got stopped. Plus attorney fees. And don't I know about the jump in insurance premiums?"

Carter begins to wonder, should he take his drink somewhere else? Perhaps one of the few open booths on the far wall? Trouble is, if he does, he might not be seen by someone entering from the outside lobby.

"Unkefer," the man says.

"I beg your pardon?"

"Name's Unkefer."

"Burns," Carter responds, but he ignores the offer to shake hands. "David Burns."

"Didn't I just read something about you in the papers?" Unkefer lifts his shaggy brows. "Something to do with vending machines."

Carter glances toward the bartender, hoping for help in getting Unkefer focused elsewhere, but the bartender is nodding intently to something being spoken into his ear by a conspiratorial-looking redhead in a tight tank top, a shimmering aqua, even in the dim light.

"Listen," Carter tells Unkefer, "I don't mean to be rude, but I've got a lot on my mind, and I need to think a few things through."

"Isn't that the way of it?" Unkefer's voice resonates with a sad wisdom.

"I'm sorry, I don't follow you."

"Man goes out to have a few drinks, think things over, maybe even formulate a plan of action. But does the universe cooperate?" Unkefer bats at his untied bow-tie. "The freaking universe has a mind of its own. Unfolds the way it wants." He takes a long sip from his ale glass and dabs at the foam moustache it has left above his lips. "You may want privacy, but the universe has spoken."

After Unkefer's pronouncement, the bartender sets a fresh glass of Newcastle ale in front of Carter. "I didn't order this," Carter tells him.

"Complements of some lady in the back." The bartender winks. "Said to give the distinguished hunk at the end of the bar a refill on what he's been drinking."

"Did she now?" Carter feels a warmth on the edge of forbidden course through him. "Well, well, well. Please thank the lady very much and ask her if she'd like to join me."

He is visualizing his handiwork, how she'll look: every item of her clothing. Erotic, but not overdone, just enough to get him going. And his outfit—black turtleneck sweater from Nordstrom's. Houndstooth jacket, and tassel loafers but no socks. Her choice for him. Have to remember that outfit.

Carter feels such a stirring now that he no longer minds the tightness of skimpy underwear she bought for him. He takes a leisurely pull at his Newcastle. When Cissy sits next to him, he will follow the scenario exactly as they'd planned.

Not a hint of recognition. Play it through right to the end. Strangers meeting in a bar. Turned on by the sight of each other. Oh, yeah. Caught up in the immediacy of the moment.

Carter can get with this program. Things are going well now. The sight of Cissy in her outfit and heels will make everything perfect. After, when they are in the motel and finished, deconstructing the event, he will be sure to congratulate her for adding the one wrinkle to the plan he'd agreed to for the sake of appearances.

"Here it comes, man," Unkefer says in a low mutter. "I just know it; your dreams will never be the same."

In spite of himself, Carter is beginning to like the man, but he does not have time to respond, thanks to his awareness of a musky cologne and then a low, throaty whisper behind him. "We might do better over there at a booth. By the way, I'm Trish."

"Okay then, Trish. I'm David." Carter turns to face her, ready to savor the effect of his creation, a velveteen moss green dress, ending just above the knees, sheer nylons, and high-heeled sandals with straps crossing around her ankles. But she is not Cissy, not even close. She has thick, wild coils of reddish orange hair with streaks and smears like a tortoiseshell cat. Her topaz eyes are made prominent by a penciling of dark liner. Thin lips open to set off what Carter guesses to be thousands of dollars worth of white, even teeth. She is the one Carter had noticed earlier, wearing the bright aqua tank top.

Even though Trish is wearing plain black flats, she is nearly as tall as Carter. "Well," she says, "you look even better up close, David. I've always had a thing for an older man."

"David's not older," Unkefer ventures from his position at the bar, "he's stunned".

Trish's eyes lock onto Carter. "Nothing to it," she says, looping her arm through his. "I'm going to take David off to a booth with me and get him unstunned."

While Trish is leading him through a scattering of tables and across a small dance floor toward the booths, Carter notices the small yellow tea rose tattooed on her left shoulder. This discovery, added to the sculpted, lanky intensity of her, begins to interest Carter in spite of the fact of her being so different from Cissy.

"Nice to know where I stand," Trish says, motioning him to

sit in the empty booth. "I can already see that you like my tat-too."

Carter follows her gaze. "Well—" he says. He sits and tries to deflect attention from an irrepressible blush by taking a sip of his Newcastle.

"It's an Achilles Gunther," she says. "His work is special." No sooner is Trish at his side, her thigh resting against his, when Unkefer appears at the table. "Condoms," he says.

Trish holds up a hand. "Not to worry, Sport. I travel pre-pared."

"No, no," Unkefer insists. "Not that." He points at Carter. "It finally came to me. You were in some kind of flap involving coin-operated vending machines. At some fancy prep school, wasn't it? Santa Ynez. Selling condoms and all. Big stink in the *News-Press* and *The Independent*. David Burns, right?"

"Hoo boy," Carter groans an inward warning.

He feels Trish's hand, kneading into his thigh. "Is that true, Sweetie? How cool! I just picked the condom king out of a roomful of strangers."

"Listen," Carter says, "there's an explanation for this."

"Is there now?" a voice surges from behind Unkefer. "Is there really an explanation for this?"

This time Carter's groan is externalized, his simultaneous lament and otherwise unutterable response to the vision of Cis-sy standing before him, wearing the garments of his choice. The knee-length moss green dress with its scoop neck enhances her posture and the slenderness of her legs as she attempts stability on heels as high as Carter dared suggest. "That's one explana-tion I'd very much like to hear, Mr.King of the Condoms."

— 🐾 —

"So you know how it looks, do you?" Cissy plunks down on the edge of one of the two beds in the motel room, knees splayed, arms thrust out behind her like tent poles. "Then maybe you can explain it to me, Jack. How *does* it look?"

"I didn't say it would be *easy* to explain," Carter chuckles at the wry nature of his observation. The fact of there being two beds in the room is yet another omen of things gone wrong here, way beyond their intended purpose and leading to the precarious terrain of confrontation. Carter tries to keep a part of his mind on the way they'd planned for things to be. There is a moment of comfort in this vision as he notices the flicker of the scented votive candles on one of the night stands, but the moment quickly recedes. "I was agreeing with the picture you must have of things."

"You're awfully damned agreeable tonight. Is that what you were doing when the redhead had her hand on your thigh, agreeing?"

"I know how it must look."

Cissy leans forward, stands with some difficulty, then ventures a few wobbly steps toward the vanity counter near the bathroom. "What it looks like to me," she says, "is a middle-aged man starting to turn kinky."

"That isn't fair, Cissy. You're in this, too. You're just as much a part of this as I am."

After another halting step, Cissy frowns, stops, lowers herself onto the vanity stool. She crosses a leg over her knee, something Carter had hoped for her to do in another context. To his expanding sense of sorrowful inevitability, she begins to unbuckle the thin strap originating at the heel line of her shoe before winding sinuously about her ankle. His sense of loss and erotic deflation becomes so severe that he cannot bear to watch her repeat the process with her right foot. He turns away from the performance to secure himself a Diet Pepsi from the honor snack fridge.

Carter drinks unwanted cola. He looks at mass-produced seascapes which have been fixed to the wall with screws. They portray no sea he has ever known, rather a bland, impersonal attempt to be pleasant. Behind him he hears the soft plop of Cissy's shoe hitting the carpeting.

"I suppose," she says, "I could have it worse".

Carter turns to regard her again, a mere mortal now, massaging her toes in relief, instead of the long-legged, sexually-

117

charged vision of his fantasies, giving off hidden sparks. When she is aware of having his attention, she continues. "Some of the women in my group, their husbands need certain incentives to keep their interests going."

"What kind of incentives?"

"Garments," Cissy says with a sigh of impatience. "Devices. Even products. Shall we mention special attentions?" She engages Carter with a lingering eye contact that makes him squirm, as much from the awareness that he wants her more than ever as from his sense of where this line of conversation will take them.

"That's why I consider myself well off. My friend, Pamela? To hear her tell it, a mild foot fetish is way down on the list, compared to her husband. You're practically normal, Jack. How are you with that?"

"How am I with that?" Carter says. "How am I? I'll tell you how I am. It's that damned awareness and sensitivity group of yours that's screwed things up. You were pretty happy before you started in with all that. You even said so yourself. The minute I try to be a little creative, add a little variety for us in our lovemaking, I get, 'You're practically normal, Jack.' You want to know how I am? That's how I am, Cissy, practically normal."

Cissy does not respond, at least not verbally for a while. She blows out each of the candles, adding the smell of scorched and smoking wick to the heavy atmosphere between them. "Sometimes you seem to forget that those groups we belong to are sources of clients." Then she begins rummaging in her overnight bag. "Well, we do have the room," she says drawing out an abbreviated nightie, then scowling at it. "We might as well use it. But don't go getting your hopes up."

Carter cannot remember the last time things had reached such a low point between them. He has difficulty sorting out all the causes contributing to the malaise that keeps him company now, perched on the side of his bed, the distance between their beds, however slight, an enormous chasm. The drinks from the early part of the evening have begun to turn on him, seeming more like invaders, their faces blackened, wearing knit watch caps, slipping through his defenses. The replay of his encounter with Trish rumbles through him like a bad inflight meal, leaving him to wrestle with his image of Cissy, before and after she'd begun to undress.

Later, in the darkness, Carter listens for sounds that will confirm one way or another whether Cissy has found the way into sleep or is still awake, nursing her displeasure at him. "Listen," he says, miserable, defeated, in a sexual funk he has not known for perhaps thirty years, "I just want you to know this one thing. The game we decided to play and the things we agreed to wear for each other, they don't mean anything compared to what I feel for you."

He waits for an answer, but there is nothing, no sound of her breathing, no flutter of sheets from her side of the room, only a long, heavy silence during which it is possible he may have drifted into sleep. He becomes aware of the whoosh of traffic from outside the room and then a woman's plaintive voice, sounding as disturbed as he feels. "Ah, Joseph, can't you wait for that until we get inside?"

Carter tries to visualize the woman and the activity she is trying to forestall. He is not sure whether to feel sympathy for her or communion for Joseph, whomever he may be and for what connection he seeks. In so doing, he acknowledges the possibility that he has drifted into sleep again. After a time, he hears his name being called. He is aware of a weight on the edge on his bed.

"I've been thinking about what you said," Cissy whispers into his ear. "It was dear of you, and I believe you. I was angry before, and my feelings were hurt, but the truth is, Jack, the truth is, until you started up with that person, I liked what we were doing." She pauses for a moment, then nudges him. "Do you understand? I very much like having you look at me the way you did. I like you in that turtleneck sweater. I'm sorry I made fun of you."

— 🐾 —

Carter can't help admiring the results of his handiwork as he watches David Burns bantering with the waitress while they

119

wait at The Wine Bistro for Cissy to appear. They are at a patio table where Burns is using just the right amount of restraint, indicating his awareness of the big-boned Nordic attractiveness of the waitress, but not bowled over by it nor at a loss for words.

"Nice tat," Burns ventures, nodding recognition of the artful rendering of a small butterfly on her shoulder. "You get that locally?"

The waitress eyes Burns for a moment. Carter can almost hear the shift from her professional attitude to a more personal appraisal. One small step for the kid, a giant step for the efforts he and Cissy have put in on him. "Gunther," she says. "Achilles Gunther."

"I thought it might be," Burns concedes. "No one gets tones the way he does."

The waitress takes it with a quick smile. She's watching Burns, maybe even deciding to work him a bit to see how he takes it. "Would you," she asks, " like to hear our today's specials?"

"I think I'd like to look some more." Burns gives the menu a bit of a flutter but keeps his eyes right on the waitress, letting her see he's enjoying the flirt. Kid couldn't have done that six months ago, before Carter and Cissy took him under their wing, started coaching him. He'd have made his play right then and probably would have overdone it later with a conspicuously big tip, blowing any chance he might have had. "Meanwhile, I'd like a Campari and soda."

Good call, Carter thinks, ordering a small bottle of Prosecco for himself. He gives the waitress a nod of dismissal so that Burns can get on with whatever was on his mind when he'd called earlier, asking if they could meet before Cissy arrived.

"The damnedest thing happened," Burns says, "and I need your take on it after the way things have been going so well for me lately."

Carter waves him on.

"Okay, this gal calls me. Never saw her before. Had no idea who she was."

"Didn't I tell you to expect that kind of thing? When you tell them you're in sales and commodities, forget about vending machines, aren't things going to happen? Commodities has an aura of mystery about it. Could be anything. Vending machines is—well, vending machines. Gum balls. Candy." He grimaces. "Condoms."

Burns nods vigorously. "That's the funny thing. This gal, she seems to know all about me. Even jokes about that business with the condom machines causing such a flap. Asks if I want to meet for drinks. So I took your and Cissy's advice, picked a place that would send the right message. The Stone Cellar at the San Ysidro Ranch."

"Excellent choice," Carter says.

"What I don't understand—the thing that baffles me is," David Burns ventures, "there I am at the bar, positioned so I can see who comes in, and I see her, at least there's this person, and she's looking expectant, and she's provocative looking enough. I hope it's her, so I say, 'Trish?'"

"Trish?" Carter says.

"Yeah, Trish. Then she looks right at me and she says, 'What do *you* want?' like she—"

"No." Carter says. "Not like. As. You understand? Since it's just the two of us, I can say this. You'll have Cissy climbing all over your ass, you use 'like' that way. As fucking though......"

"As though I—" He pauses for a moment. "—were some leper. So I told her, 'I'm David Burns.' and she said 'Bullshit you're David Burns. You don't look anything like David Burns. What *is* this?' And I said 'What is *what?*' And she—"

Burns' voice trails off. His perplexed expression is replaced by an expansive grin. "Oh, wow." Burns has forfeited the detached suavity he'd demonstrated with the waitress. "Wow," Burns says, standing with alacrity.

Carter gets a scent of tangy verbena cologne, then sees a shadow fall on to the table in front of him. Cissy has arrived.

He feels intimidated into standing by the enthusiasm of Burns's response, which he more appreciates now that he can see Cissy. She's worn the floral-pattern chintz dress before, but somehow there is less of it and more of Cissy, as though points

121

of interest had been framed. A noticeable touch of cleavage, a belted waist giving emphasis to her hips, and the shoes from what Carter has begun to think of as The Great Motel Fiasco. Cissy catches his scrutiny and flashes him a wink. "How are my two favorite men doing?"

"We were just reviewing some fine points of David's social life," Carter offers. He notes that Burns has still not recovered his cool. In fact, Burns's jaw has started to go slack when he greets Cissy. "Wow," he says. "You sure look—"

"I look what?" Cissy says, taking a seat between them.

It is almost pathetic the way Burns looks at him, as if asking permission. "Sexy," he says, then begins to redden and takes a sip of his Campari.

But Cissy will not let the matter rest. "You think so?"

Burns can't return her glance, causing Carter to suspect it was the cleavage that got to him.

"Yeah." Burns takes another sip, all but ignoring the waitress when she returns to take their lunch orders.

The rest of the session is a disaster. Burns appears to have regressed or at least lost his edge, showing little or no interest in the social events Cissy is suggesting for him, a mere nod of response to her urging him to join the Chamber of Commerce, and not showing much enthusiasm for any of Carter's suggestions for business strategies. Burns seems preoccupied, almost possessed.

Twice Carter catches him at furtive, sidelong glances in Cissy's direction, convincing him it is indeed the cleavage. Well, to each his own. He is more drawn to the supple grace of Cissy's limbs, or the unconscious mannerism she has of turning up her lower lip when she is amused. But no accounting for taste.

After another hour, it is Burns who brings lunch to an end. "I guess," he says, "I'd better get back to work. Two shopping malls and a five-theatre cineplex to cover. Lots of vending machines."

On the positive side, Carter notices that when the tattooed waitress brings the bill, she gives it to Burns, and Carter manages to catch that she's put her phone number on back of the cash register tape.

"Can I give you a lift back to your office?" Burns asks Cissy.

"What a lovely suggestion," Cissy says.

Right, Carter thinks. Lovely. "I'll take her," he says. "It's out of your way."

"I don't mind," Burns says.

"I've got some errands along the way," Cissy says, standing, " I think I'll walk."

"In those heels?"

Cissy smiles at him. "They're what got me here in the first place, aren't they?"

— ❧ —

Carter tries to balance conflicting suspicions. Either he has a few fences to mend with Cissy or she has something in the works with Burns, in which case he may have a great many fences to mend with Cissy. "Listen," he tells Burns, "I wouldn't worry about the experience you had with that Trish person. There's probably some simple explanation."

Burns shakes his head. "I'd sure like to get to the bottom of it. Why would she be so sure I'm not me?"

Carter gives him a buddy poke. "Take if from the coach here." He points at the cash register strip with the waitress's phone number on it. "You're better off dealing with the tangible."

By the time he gets his car out of the parking lot and has driven toward Cissy's office, she's covered the distance and come into possession of a shopping bag from an El Paseo boutique, giving credibility to her plea of an errand. When she responds to his tap of the horn, he says, "We have to talk."

She does not seem the slightest bit defensive when she approaches him, causing Carter to begin an immediate inventory of fences to be mended. "I thought you had a meeting," she says.

"It can wait."

"In which case," Cissy says, coming around to Carter's side, "move over. I'll drive."

Within moments, she has made a precipitous u-turn, headed for the southbound freeway ramp. "What was going on with you back there, Jack?" She accelerates onto the freeway then heads south, toward Summerland. When Carter does not answer her question, she persists. "Is there something between you and David, some dynamic I'm not getting?"

"I was thinking some dynamic between *you* and David. He couldn't keep his eyes off your—"

"I *know*," she interrupts. 'Who would have thought that about him?" Before Carter can respond, she laughs and says "I guess *you* thought that about him. You were jealous, weren't you?"

"Come on, Cissy. He's our client."

"You *were*. You still are. I can see it. What a turn-on. Twenty-three years, and you still get jealous. An absolute turn-on." She exits at the Summerland ramp, turns right toward the beach, but veers off before the entrance to the park, traversing the unpaved frontage road. "I'll admit I was toying with the notion of first base when he offered me a ride."

"First base? People still use that term?"

"It's what you got on our first date. Unhooked bra."

"That's second base."

She pulls off the frontage road, then crosses the railroad tracks onto a plateau overlooking the beach, where she parks and turns toward him.

"Look at you. You're all—"

"All what?"

"I *said* toying, Jack. Men aren't the only ones who fantasize. Anyhow, it's all worked to your benefit. Your jealousy is much more interesting to me than any notion of first base with David Burns."

"I am not goddamned jealous, Cissy."

"Here," she says, extending a hand toward her cleavage. "Second base for you already."

— ❧ —

The tide is out, offering a choice of walking south to Fernald Point or as far north as the harbor and breakwater, and with it an awareness of limitless options. They walk toward the sun, now dropping down toward hills of The Mesa, where it will disappear. Along the shoreline, Carter feels a dizzying sense of mischief and pleasure, a kind of spiritual boosterism, the sort of hopeful vision he encourages in his clients.

He smiles at the inventory of his love life with Cissy. There have been very few hitches or speed bumps. The abandon with which they'd just had each other seems to portend a new plateau for them, an even greater horizon of companionable intimacy. Instinct tells him this is not a time to discuss such things or, for that matter, any words at all, only a contemplative interior celebration. This euphoria is borne even further along when Cissy reaches for his hand.

After they have walked along for a few paces, she begins to hum. Carter luxuriates in the sound of it until Cissy becomes the first to speak.

"You remember that melody, don't you?" she asks.

"Piece of cake," Carter says. "The major theme from *Symphony in D* by Caesar Franck."

"It is *not*." Cissy stops. "It's *Peter and the Wolf*."

"I know *Peter and the Wolf* when I hear it. *Peter and the Wolf* goes dum dah, de dum da de dah—"

"That's what I was humming."

Carter gives a toss of his head. "You were going dah de dah dum dah de dah. That's the Franck."

"How gross." Cissy abruptly lets go of his hand. "The Franck symphony is called *The Organ Symphony*."

"Well, yes, there is an organ in it," Carter says, sensing he has somehow begun to lose ground. "Franck was an organist. It makes perfect sense for him to have used one in a symphony."

"You're making fun of it."

"Sweetie, I am *not* making fun. How am I making fun?"

"The first time we ever made love, in the same place where we just made love, you had the radio on, and the music was *Peter and the Wolf*."

"Hoo boy," Carter says.

"It was something special to me. I was one of the few in my sorority who didn't have that association with Ravel's *Bolero*. It made me feel different."

"Hoo boy," Carter says.

Cissy stands hipshot in the moist sand, wheeling gulls contesting the afternoon airspace with *recitatives* of complaint. "Is that all you can say, Mr. Communications Expert? Is that the sum of your feelings on the matter?"

"Hoo boy."

— 🐚 —

"Aren't you guys a little old to be getting into this?" Their inquisitor lifts his thin, almost-continuous brow line. With great purpose, he selects a red M & M candy from a bowl in front of him. "I mean, it is your first time, isn't it?"

"Is there something wrong with that?" Carter asks.

Chewing his M & M with deliberation, the man replies. "Never too late to start, but you have to ask yourself why you waited all this time."

"You make us sound old," Cissy says.

The man surveys Cissy for a moment, nods, then smiles. "I'd say handsome. Old for this."

Carter senses the beginnings of a bristling reaction in Cissy.

"Isn't handsome something associated with masculine features?" She counters.

"Handsome and bright," the man says. Now he winks. "Used to being thought of as attractive. Maybe even beautiful. Perhaps a tad resentful of being thought of as a trophy wife."

"More than a tad, mister." Cissy is close to making a bark of it. Carter thinks, but does not say, hoo boy. He looks at the room again, trying to square it with his preconceived notions of what it would be. The room is a small rectangle, its walls a flat Navajo white. On one wall is a splashy Diebenkorn, opposite it a Motherwell, somehow achieving a cheering effect from somber colors. He and Cissy are on a taupe-colored love seat facing Achilles Gunther, a small, knobby man who sits behind a small library table on which there is, in addition to the bowl of

M & M candies, a note pad and a bud vase with one Belle of Portugal rose. Carter suspects there are at least two other rooms in the suite.

It surprises Carter that Gunther's office is located in the upper village shopping square, just a few doors from a bank where the minimum beginning account is $10,000, and between a hair salon and luggage shop. It also surprises him that Gunther's only sign is a small, framed cardboard bearing his initial, AG, embossed in a type face resembling the one used on American currency.

Gunther seems to be aware of and amused by Carter's sense of anomaly. "We are all individuals, Mr. Carter, unless we opt to follow class or party lines." He toys with another red M & M. "Not all tattoo parlors look like mine. I have never tattooed a Marine, nor have I tattooed an anchor on a sailor. So far as I'm aware, I've never tattooed an individual who was intoxicated. You have no idea how much more difficult it is to tattoo someone who's been drinking. Alcohol gets the blood right up close to the skin."

"I don't see any tattoos on you," Cissy ventures.

"You'd be surprised at how many tattoos are not readily visible, Mrs. Carter. Would it help if I told you I'm not the dancer; I'm the dance?" He pops the M & M into his mouth. "But this is all academic, isn't it? You're wondering if you have the courage to go through with this, testing out your objections, looking for some reason to get up and leave, looking for fly-stained equipment or some compelling last-minute argument against the impulse that brought you here. Well, allow me to give you something to consider. It is, in fact, a condition of my agreeing to tattoo you."

"A disclaimer, right?" Carter asks.

"No such thing." Gunther rises, making them aware once again of how short he is. "I'm going to give you some time—say ten minutes—to think about where, Mr. Carter, you'd like me to tattoo your wife, what point on that admirable body of hers. And then I want you, Mrs. Carter, to tell me where on your husband's body you would get the most pleasure from seeing a tattoo. I won't tattoo just one of you. Both or—" He snaps his fingers. "Nada."

Gunther bows, smiles, and makes a few adjustments on his chronometer watch. "I hope you realize how fortunate you both are," he says with another bow. "Ten minutes, then," he says, striding toward the door.

"What do you think he meant by that?" Cissy asks when Gunther has shut the door behind him. "Is he bragging about how good he is, how we shouldn't miss this big chance?"

"Are you getting cold feet, Cissy?"

"Did you see the way he looked at me?"

"Pretty much the way David looked at you."

Cissy stands and begins to move around Gunther's desk. "David didn't want to tattoo me."

"He hasn't even got to first base yet. Remember?"

Cissy flashes a look of irritation, but she quickly recovers and deflects it. "Okay, Jack. Where would you like for me to be tattooed? And no fair dodging. I asked first."

Carter sees the glow on Cissy's face, reminding him of her expression as she drove them to Lookout Point above the beach in Summerland. He is feeling his own face beginning to tingle from the curiosity about where Cissy would like him to be tattooed. It comes to him that they have never discussed what images or figures would be used if they were to go through with this. He begins to consider places and possibilities.

"What?" Cissy says.

"Peter." Carter fakes a Russian accent while smiling at her. "Peter and de wool-uf." He pauses for emphasis. "Dum day, de dum de dah."

Messages

This was their first time in Dana's bedroom during daylight hours. Roger Beck had been in Dana's bedroom before, but always at night, when they'd been drinking and fooling around enough to make them excited to be here. Today, there'd been no drinking or what Dana called canoodling.

Today's venture started with a pause in an ordinary conversation, a glance between them, and a smile of consent. Dana's bedroom had a theme, a goddamn motif. The drapes, bedspread, and the cushions of a small settee were variations of a chintz pattern.

Her personal things—picture frames, books, dressing table toiletries—were quite well organized in comparison to the freeform clutter of the living room, and he saw the invisible hand of The Therapist, Dr. Conrad, supporting her need for order in her intimate surroundings but directing her to dare to be disorganized in public. To top it off, the shadows revealed a thin downy intrusion of blonde fuzz on her upper lip. She might even use wax or some other painful method to remove it. The knowledge caused him to feel irresistibly drawn to her.

Dana stirred at the tickle of his lips on her shoulder and was immediately aroused again, caught in the drama of the chemistry between them.

"I'll tell," Beck said.

She ran her fingertips over his thigh, laughing at the shiver this caused him. "What are you talking about?"

"The secrets. The atomic secrets." He shivered again. "I'll even throw in the code and the message drops," he said. "The M stands for Morley."

There was a hoarse seriousness in her whisper. "You really mean it, don't you? You're making light of it because you're so serious."

"Mild mannered M. Roger Beck is really a Morley."

Dana seemed to be looking for a place to begin. "Sometimes I binge out on martial arts movies," she said. "I rent five or six, buy the budget pack of Snickers candy bars, and watch non-stop."

"I'm not really poor," he said. "I used to be, but not any-more."

"I don't have to work at that library where you met me. I get upwards of five hundred dollars each for my architectural watercolors."

Beck focused on the curve of her hip and then on an irra-tional splash of gray in her otherwise brown hair. "I'm still mar-ried. But it's nothing to be concerned about; I only did it in the first place so she could get a green card."

"I have a daughter, Frances. She just had her first period. She's very excited."

"I don't want to lose you. That's why I waited until now to tell you about Claudine."

"I figure I'm a year older than you, and—"

"And—?"

"I don't want to lose you, either, no matter what the 'M' stands for."

"When I first saw you knitting I got so turned on by the way your fingers moved that I had to look away."

"I rented a whole bunch of Bruce Lee movies that night," Dana said.

"I've seen women knit before and that never happened to me. I wonder what it is."

A smile of such unrelenting mischief played into Dana's lips that Beck began to fear for the effectiveness of his squash game scheduled for later. "I'll bet I can show you," she said.

— 🍂 —

Beck's first impression of Frances was a girl mortified by her relative tallness, a sprinkle of freckles on her high-boned cheeks, and the need for braces to correct an overbite. She seemed so grounded in the present moment that Beck was sure she had no idea of the overpowering effect she would soon have on boys of her own age — the same melting, primal reach her mother had on him.

"I was very surprised when Mama told me we were all going to live together," Frances said.

They were standing in an empty three-bedroom, two-and-a-half-bath condo the brokerage firm for which Beck was an agent was having a particularly difficult time selling or leasing.

"Why were you surprised?" Beck noticed Dana had begun to redden.

"Mama said you two were having great sex, but frankly, Mama has a hard time keeping boyfriends to the point where that even matters. It always works out that she tries to disguise her intelligence."

"How'd you like to see the room that's going to be yours, honey?" Dana said. "You even have a separate entrance."

"Are there contiguous walls?" Frances asked. "Am I to be next to you?"

Beck, who had shown this condo a number of times, thumped the walls with brio. "Lath and plaster," he said, "and sound proof. So even though the answer is yes, there is, as they say, no problem."

Frances showed him the full extent of her braces with a wide smile. "That's a relief. As I'm sure you've noticed, Mama can be very loud when she makes love."

"There's even a little patch for you to garden, honey," Dana said, "and there's no reason why you can't have a cat."

"May I call you Roger?" Frances asked. "I'm sure we'll get

131

along. I'm not a brat, I'm just — weird. I've started hearing voices, you know."

"Unh, no," Beck said. "I guess I didn't."

"We've got to get you to your music lesson, honey," Dana said. "I just wanted you to see where we're going to live and to assure you we're in the same district, so you won't have to change schools."

Frances linked her arm through Beck's. "Right now," she said, "the voices are telling me to raise an army."

— 𝕚 —

While it was true that Charlie Mitchell was known among his close friends as an unrelenting blowhard given to outbursts and postures designed to provoke confrontations, Beck nevertheless found himself surprised and annoyed as he became a target of the Charlie Mitchell opportunity.

Mitchell had, in fact, just used a cocktail wiener, impaled on a toothpick, to call attention to Beck's departure from the back table at The Grill where he, Beck, and four others had been in convivial disarray for nearly an hour, leaving a detritus of foreign beer bottles, peanut casings, and damp cocktail napkins filled with the scribbling and numbers of Important Computations. "Wait a minute," Charlie Mitchell said, impeding Beck's path from the table. "Let me get this straight. You are leaving our company for the expressed purpose of calling Dana?"

Mitchell now had the focus of the four other revelers, and Beck, still not sure of what was coming, had the feeling of a man who had just stepped in dog droppings, and was now trying to avoid similar booby traps of Nature. "I thought it would be considerate, under the circumstances."

The cocktail wiener, like a conductor's baton, signaled a forthcoming effect. "You are calling Dana to get permission to have another round with your colleagues?"

"I'm doing no such thing, Charlie. Since when do I need permission to have drinks with friends? I'm calling because this is our first night of —"

"Of?" Mitchell gave an exaggerated tug at his suede vest.

"Of living together. Dana, her kid, and me. I just want us to get off on the right foot."

"I rest my case." Mitchell plopped the cocktail wiener into his mouth and managed to convey to the group a sense of malicious satisfaction from the way he chewed. "No further questions."

"Goddamn it, Charlie, you take a simple, considerate gesture and turn it into a—"

Mitchell made maximum use of his voice. "You are pussy-whipped."

"Goddamn it, Charlie."

"The kid probably has her own cell phone, in her own name."

"I don't see what's so remarkable about that."

"Pussy-whipped." Mitchell grinned satisfaction to the jury of four, including Lola Kelly, whose quarterly sales commissions were the envy of all of them. "I leave it to the vote," Mitchell taunted.

Cries of "Pussy-whipped! Pussy-whipped!" trailed after Beck in his hegira from the table. He sought the corner near the restrooms, where the outlines of old pay phones remained, ghostly reminders of another era.

He waited, iPhone in hand, for the mechanical voice of the Siri Operating System to speak to him. "Call home," he told it. Her. Whatever.

"Roger home? Or Roger and Dana home?"

"Jesus," Beck said. "Roger and Dana."

Soon, he heard the sound of Dana's recorded voice. "You've reached the residence of M. Roger Beck and Dana McKay. We're sorry we can't take your call, but neither of us is in right now. Please leave us a message. We really want to hear what you have to tell us. We'll call back as soon as we can."

It was not so much the message, although Beck had found himself cringing at that in two places; it was more the sound of a smugness, of some inherent nesting DNA Beck had not previously detected in Dana that rankled him. As he returned to the table where his friends awaited him, he knew that he must take a strict control of the outgoing message on the machine. If Charlie Mitchell were to hear such a message, life would become hell in a new meaning of the word.

"Ah, back already, are we?" Mitchell observed. "Let me get you a drink to celebrate your new arrangement. Waitress, a Shirley Temple for my friend here."

— 🐾 —

Dana's hatchback, its rear deck agape, stood before the front door, a jaunty, four-wheeled cornucopia of what Dana quickly termed provisions, essentials, and basics, which she was taking into the kitchen.

"It was so romantic getting your message," she said, looking with satisfaction at a packet of shitake mushrooms. "Our first incoming phone call, and it's you, being considerate."

Frances appeared, nodded cordially, and began to help sort through the incoming groceries, arranging them on the shelves in what Beck decided was a display of uncommonly sophisticated functionality until he realized that her driving motivation was a search for particular items. An accusatory note, the first he'd heard from her, crept into her voice. "Did you forget my stuff?"

Dana's response reminded Beck of the smugness inherent in her tape recorded message. Nothing was going to daunt her. "It's right here, kiddo." She set a ten-pound jute sack of brown rice on the counter next to Frances, followed in quick succession by a large bottle of soya sauce, a jar of tahini mix, a sack of lentils, and an enormous jar of peanut butter.

"Orders from headquarters," Frances explained.

"Headquarters?" Beck said.

"Yeah, the voices. No meat for a while." She shrugged. "I've got to detox. They want to make sure I get all their communications."

"I brought home some Chinese take-out to celebrate our first night," Beck said. "You can eat that, can't you?"

Frances closed her eyes for a moment as if meditating.

134

"There's sweet and sour shrimp, vegetable chow yuk, kung pao chicken, moo goo gai pan, and pork spareribs."

Frances brightened. "Everything's cool," she said, "but the moo goo gai pan and spare ribs."

"Watch this space," Beck said, "for an important message."

Frances giggled. "They like you."

"Can we get this stuff put away?" Dana handed Beck a large shopping bag from a department store.

In the bag, Beck found two packets of paper cocktail napkins that had been imprinted: Roger and Dana. Below them were thick, shaggy wash cloths and face towels.

"Frances gets her own set," Dana said," and the bath sheets won't be ready until next week."

"Ready?" Then Beck discovered what she meant. The wash cloths and face towels had been given monograms, his and Dana's initials fancifully entwined within the outline of a heart.

"You don't like it," Dana said. "I can tell from looking at you."

Beck, who earlier that week had spent twenty minutes with a razor blade, removing an alligator from a new polo shirt, said, "That's taking my response a bit to the extreme."

"I just wanted it to be nice for us." Dana hurriedly left the room as tears began to form in her eyes.

"You would think—" Frances said.

"You would think what?"

"That she'd learn by now. I'll put that stuff in the oven because you're going to need about an hour to make up, and then she'll probably want to take a shower. But I hope you don't mind if I have some of that kungpao chicken in the mean time."

When Beck ordered his last round before departing The Grill, his companions joined him in switching from beer to the more bracing effects of cognac.

"You have to face the fact," Charlie Mitchell warned, "that the child may not be merely going through a phase—but is truly endowed with an extraordinary talent."

His pronouncement caused an uneasy silence. Once, as Lola Kelly perused *The New York Times* Sunday crossword puzzle, stumbling over 24 down—an avatar of Vishnu—wasn't it Charlie who, without missing a beat, had said, "If it's four letters, it's Rama, and if it's seven, it's gotta be Krishna"? And wasn't it also Charlie who could identify by name the bearded, sometimes turbaned sages depicted in the lotus position? Or the fierce-looking dark-skinned goddess who wore a necklace of human skulls?

"Just what I need," Beck said.

"Look at it this way," said Gonder, who had a small one-man office with the designation "$$$ Inc." lettered on the only door, and who was variously thought by them to be a CIA-backed front organization, a money-laundering operation, a mail order genius, or All of the Above. As Charlie Mitchell put it, "Everyone has some kind of problem."

"My boyfriend—two boyfriends back—had a real problem with black underwear. After a while, things got very difficult for me." Lola Kelly shook her head at the memory.

"My first wife," Charlie Mitchell confessed, "took things. Small, pocketable souvenirs. When I confronted her, she likened what she did to the Native American Plains Indians and their practice of counting coup. We once stopped for a snack at the airport before catching a flight to San Francisco, and she was caught by the metal detector."

"This is not the kind of problem I have experience with." Beck found neither answer nor solace in his drink.

"All right," Mitchell said. "Wait it out. Take a pragmatic approach. But meanwhile, you've got to create a diversion. You say the teacher who's coming to tea is English?"

Beck nodded. "Miss Hayward. Yes."

"Up the street is the Xanadu Coffee Shop," Charlie Mitchell counseled. "Deluge Miss Hayward in pastries. Eclairs. Napoleons. Linzer torte. Even Baklava, if they have it. The English love having to make choices."

"But for God's sake, chew some cloves," Lola Kelly said, "or she'll think you've been drinking."

— ❧ —

Beck was disturbed to discover he had either misheard the time of Miss Hayward's arrival or had followed some psychological vector in drinking past it, leaving Dana to cope with her alone for the better part of half an hour. His awareness of the need for at least one demonstration of contrition was expanded when he noted that Dana had managed to produce brewed tea, scones, petits fours, and English clotted cream, on top of which his boxes of pastries from the Xanadu seemed to him like an attempt at ransom.

"We were talking about the voices Frances hears," Dana said, trying, Beck thought, to sound a bit too casual.

Miss Hayward, an agreeably middle-aged woman with a cultivated but not excessive Received Standard English, and unruly blonde curls, lifted her tea cup in salute to Beck. "She's quite clear on who they are," she said.

"Saint Catherine, Saint Michael, and Saint Margaret." Beck was put at greater ease by the fact that Miss Hayward did not wear sensible shoes.

"Ah, I see she's told you."

"Well, no, but given the obvious parallels, I did some research." By which Beck meant he'd had a serious conversation with Charlie Mitchell.

Miss Hayward sipped her tea appreciatively and seemed to confirm the wisdom of Charlie Mitchell's strategy by adding to her plate a Napoleon, an eclair, and a custard shell topped with sliced kiwi. "I'm afraid I must tell you she hears as well from Emmanuel Swedenborg, whom she calls Manny, and Madam Blavatsky, whom she addresses as H.P.B., those being her actual initials," Miss Hayward said, wagging a finger at Beck, "and so we have complications of a sort. We must not assume that Frances is merely responding as an historical parallel or that we can diagnose this as simply as, say, a common cold or, given recent physiological events, that the dear child is undergoing some idiosyncratic form of PMS."

Beck, to whom Emmanuel Swedenborg and Madame Blavatsky were complete strangers, felt the need for a prop of some sort, a need he addressed by serving himself an eclair after inquiring about Dana's preferences, wondering if Charlie Mitchell were still at The Grill, and if he could contrive to reach Charlie for a quick briefing before Miss Hayward left.

It was then that Beck noticed the napkin Miss Hayward had been using to deftly blot pastry crumbs from the corners of her lips before returning it to her right knee. The napkin bore a monogram. Beck shot a sharper glance than intended at Dana, who recoiled in surprise, giving Beck an immediate pang of conscience. His morbid need to see the monogram was constrained by virtue of where the napkin lay, spread over Miss Hayward's demurely tilted knees.

"I think we've reached the point," Miss Hayward said, "where it is in Frances's best interests that we do something."

"Has she," Dana asked, "been disturbing the other students?"

Miss Hayward smiled. "She has attempted to enlist a few young men and a janitor to her cause, but you must understand. All students of that age are a bit— odd."

When Dana winced, Miss Hayward gave a sympathetic toss of her head. "But Frances is certainly no more noteworthy than young Geoffrey, who is quite gifted mathematically and who has begun to leave geometric theorems in the gym bags and purses of girls who have in common a notably developing bustline."

"Then I don't understand what you mean by taking action," Dana said.

Beck strained to see the monogram on Miss Hayward's napkin as she touched it again to her lips. "This will impress you as old fashioned, I know." She smiled. "When I leave, you will undoubtedly turn to your handsome and attentive Mr. Beck here and say, 'Can you imagine her old fashioned—her nineteenth-century resolution to the problem.' But I think we ought to bring Frances into the picture. In a creative way, you understand. I think we—you—ought to ask Frances if, under the circumstances, she would like to leave our school and transfer to one of a religious orientation—"

"But—" Dana said.

Beck and Miss Hayward overrode her with gestures. "— or ask her if she would like to begin religious training after school. And then I think we should all of us, me, you, and Mr. Beck, be very quiet and listen very carefully to what she tells us."

The source of Miss Hayward's napkin, a modest pile of similar ones on the table behind the tea things, was now visible to Beck; he rose to confront it. "That's very sensible," he said. "That's actually a skilled managerial response, very much like the motivational tapes I've been using."

"Do you think so, Mr. Beck? I'm flattered."

"But suppose," Dana said, "she wants a religious school."

"Jesus Christ," Beck said, reading the monogram. Tea with Roger and Dana.

"Suppose she wants to become a nun?"

"My dear," Miss Hayward said, "young Geoffrey of fabled mathematical abilities now wishes to be an landscape architect, and another of your daughter's classmates, an incipient feminist, I might add, wishes to become a professional jockey. One of the few true joys of being young and in Frances's position is the number of options available to her."

"Tea with Roger and Dana," Beck said.

"I'm glad you're taking it so well," Miss Hayward said. "Your attitude can't help but have a positive impact." She winked at Beck. "Of course we mustn't discount the possibility—"

"The possibility?" Dana said.

"—That the child has a genuine vocation." She spread her hands. "We must always leave some room at the inn for the most rational option. And now I wonder, since my own voices told me to take that splendid kiwi custard and my tummy tells me I cannot possibly deal with it at the moment, if I might have a doggie bag?"

Beck felt an overpowering sense of relief when Dana meticulously transferred the kiwi custard and an eclair into a box that bore the label of The Xanadu Coffee Shop, which left no room for other commentary.

"I couldn't help noticing your napkins," Miss Hayward said

at the door. "It's so nice to think of such a delightful young couple observing the amenities and having tea."

"Yes," Dana said nervously, "it's become a tradition."

In the darkness of their bedroom, listening to Dana's measured breathing, Beck revised a diplomatic, sideways approach borrowed from one of the sales techniques tapes, deciding instead on a frontal assault from one of die sports motivational tapes. *You are an admirable person and I love everything about you except those goddamned monograms.* That had a nice ring to it, an unvarnished presentation of facts. Perhaps the admirable part could go, even if it were true. He did admire Dana, except for those goddamned monograms. Maybe a more straightforward tack. *I have never been so turned on by anyone in my life, but couldn't we please have plain towels?*

Beck's eyes smarted from the sudden blaze of light. He sat reflexively and, in doing so, made a painful discovery. Dana had been leaning over him. His upward movement had caused them to bump heads. After a quick inventory of his responses, he began to believe he'd drowsed while Dana was saying something to him and that his lack of response had fueled Dana's ire and her need for direct confrontation.

A quaver in her voice led him to reconsider. "Admit it," she said. "You've begun to feel trapped. You're having regrets."

The scenario was clear now: he hadn't drowsed at all, nor had she said anything. She'd been waiting there in the darkness, trying to screw up her own courage to initiate contact. Turning on the light was a stage direction from Dr. Conrad, The Shrink: confront the problem in the open.

"I don't feel trapped," Beck said. "I certainly have no regrets; it simply makes me feel uneasy. It seems to represent everything I've worked so hard to overcome."

"What do people do when this happens?" She began to cry, softly, without drama. "Do you have any idea how drawn to you I am? When I first met you, I began asking Dr. Conrad about addictive personality, and when he asked me what that meant to me, I told him I know this man, Roger Beck, who

140

could possibly be chocolate, caffeine, and cigarettes all rolled up into one.

Beck couldn't tell if the shudder coursing his spine came from the tickle of her hair against his shoulder or some interior stimulus. "After we made love the first time," he said, "I stood watching you when you brushed your hair. I couldn't believe something so wonderful had happened to me."

"I've thought about sending her away to school, but I can't. I wouldn't feel right about it."

"She's taking it better than we are."

"Then what are we going to do? Dr. Conrad always tells me to focus on the thing I'm afraid of losing." She wiped at tears with the back of her hand. "What can I do to not lose you?"

There was no denying the way Dana's shoulders had a sensual sweep, or that her hair, when at its present state of dishevelment, conveyed an exciting wantonness. "Okay," Beck said. "Okay."

"Will you please stop toying with me and give me an answer?"

"Goddamn it, I'm not toying. This isn't easy."

"Do you think it's easy for me?"

"It's more difficult telling it than it ought to be. It even sounds silly. Okay. I think we ought to get rid of every towel in this place, even the paper ones, and start fresh. From now on, I should be the one—"

"Towels. This is about towels?"

"To take care of our towel needs."

"It is." Dana hefted a small tape player and threw it at Beck. "It isn't about her. It's about towels." She threw two motivational tapes at him, a clock radio, a telephone shaped like a Ferrari, a note pad and a ball point pen. "I have a daughter who is hearing voices, a psychiatrist who thinks I'm overly structured, and a lover who has a thing about towels." She moved to the book case and began throwing paperback bestsellers at Beck. When she ran out of these, she began with the Time-Life art books.

Ducking or evading the missiles directed his way, Beck

noticed the shoulder strap of Dana's nightgown was frequently slipping, exposing the entire sweep of shoulder.

Beck felt an exhilarating sense of freedom. "It's really the monograms," he said as the collected later works of Constable slammed into his chest. "I absolutely cringe when I see those monograms."

"I was afraid I was losing you," Dana said. "You let me think that." The works of Turner flew at him, as well as those of Claude Lorrain and separate volumes of Holbein the Elder and Younger. "You did, M. Roger Beck. You let me think that."

"She can probably hear us," Beck said, cocking his head toward the direction of Frances's room.

"Lath and plaster," Dana said, advancing toward him. "Knock on the walls." The hoarseness in her voice lost its edge and began to suggest a quality of smugness. "Even if she does hear us—she'll probably think it's them."

Between the Acts

What more could an actor want? Bender had been living in a 1986 Volvo 740 station wagon for nearly a month before the police found him. The Volvo was partial payment for Bender's services rendered to a dinner-theater project after the company had been forced to seek protection under Chapter Eleven of the bankruptcy code. With nearly two hundred thousand miles on the odometer, the Volvo was still mercifully free of valve clatter or cranky transmission. Bender was sharing accommodations and such amenities as there were with Taxi, a tortoise-shell tabby given him as a lover's memento nearly a year earlier by a woman named Heather.

"No wonder it took us so long to locate you," Officer Ron Magellan observed, crouching alongside the open tailgate where Bender sat. A chisel-browed man whose dark eyes seemed to reflect the ironies of his race and profession, he tapped a pocket notebook with a ballpoint pen. "Our information shows you living in an AMC Pacer."

Eager for his morning coffee before engaging in conversation, Bender had been in the process of opening a can of Nine Lives chicken-tuna-liver medley for Taxi. He shook his head. "AMC Pacer would be Unkefer."

"The writer?"

Bender nodded. "Got leanings toward Albee and Beckett. A Pacer makes sense for him."

"Tall fellow like you," Magellan ventured, "I'd think an early '90s Subaru wagon might be an attraction. Nice kitty, by the way. Okay for me to pet?"

"Can we please get to the point here?" Magellan's partner, Theodore Bordofsky, called from the black-and-white cruiser waiting at a gurgling idle. "I haven't had my morning coffee."

"Ah, the point." Magellen acknowledged as a red Geo with more spirit than roadability lurched around the corner, then parked behind the Volvo. Bender sighed at the sight of it.

"The point, Mr. Bender. The department is having a fundraiser for charity. We were thinking it would be nice to have you doing some of the more memorable speeches and soliloquies from Shakespeare. You know. Henry IV's deathbed advice to his son. And 'We happy few, we band of brothers' from *Henry V.*"

"Lear," Bordofsky called from the black-and-white. "Pray, do not mock me: I am a very foolish fond old man."

The door of the Geo opened with a groan, kicked wider by a tall young woman who swung her coltish legs to the street. She emerged carrying a Styrofoam cup of coffee and a small bakery sack. "O, look upon me, sir," she curtsied to Bordofsky. "And hold your hands in benediction o'er me."

Bender closed his eyes for a moment at the effect of her raw command of presence. "Cindy," he groaned. "What are you doing here?"

"Amazing," Bordofsky said. "That line goes right before—"

Magellan nodded appreciation when Cindy drew close enough to present the Styrofoam cup and the bakery bag to Bender with a flourish. "Thoughtful daughter you've got there, Bender. Talented, too."

"Daughter, hell," Cindy humphed. "I'm trying to become his girlfriend."

Bender pinched at the bridge of his nose.

"With all due respect," Magellen said, "isn't he a bit old for you? Got to be pushing forty."

"Boys my age," Cindy told him, "they leave me cold."

"No offense," Magellen said, "but maybe at your age, raging hormones and all, being left cold isn't such a bad idea."

"I'm nearly twenty," Cindy countered.

"Seventeen," Bender said. "Opinionated, precocious, and seventeen." Lifting the plastic lid of the cup, he saw the reassuring foam of latte. When he tasted it, he wondered how Cindy had come by his preference with such accuracy.

"So what about it, Bender?" Bordofsky called from the black-and-white. "Seeing as it's a charity thing—"

"Yeah, yeah, I know," Bender said. A charity thing meant a freebie. But as his no-nonsense pal, Wolfe, was so quick to point out, for an actor, work of any kind was work. There was always the chance that someone in the audience would become energized and want you for another project that actually paid money.

"There may be some perks in this," Magellan offered.

"Right," Bender said. "You'll let me sleep here without rousting me."

"Don't be so quick to cynicism." Magellen dropped back into a crouch, a gesture Bender catalogued with an eye to using it when he, at some time, might wish to convey confidentiality.

Magellan began to speak of a large storage facility in the sprawling industrial tract off Milpas Street, where individuals could rent space to store unused furniture, office records, even auto parts and small vending machines. "The facility is owned by a young entrepreneur named Frank Burns. A nice little cash cow, bringing in a tidy aggregate of monthly rent." Just as the character played by the actor Claude Rains in Magellan's favorite film, *Casablanca*, was shocked to discover that there was gambling in the back room of Rick's bar, Magellan was disturbed by his knowledge of occasional poker, craps, and three-card monte venues operating out of one rental unit. He was further shocked, even a bit outraged, at the implication that some of the tools in some of the storage sheds might be used in connection with a chop shop that specialized in foreign car parts, and although there was no hard evidence available, there were rumors that a twenty-five-by-twenty-five-foot unit rented by Conrad Burnaby was a trove of burglarized appliances and jewelry.

"I am not suggesting that our Frank Burns is engaged in any illegal activities," Magellan explained. "But it seems to me that he might want the security of having someone live in the small watchman's apartment, just to forestall any suspicious behavior, if you get my drift."

"I get your drift," Bender said. "If I do the show, you'll have a chat with Burns, and I'll get the apartment."

"You'll love the neighborhood," Bordofsky called. "Close to inexpensive Mexican restaurants and bakeries. Now can we please get out of here? The smell of that coffee is getting to me."

When the two policemen were gone, Cindy perched next to Bender on the rear deck of the Volvo, watching him sip his coffee. She waited until he delved into the bakery sack to remove a croissant. "Strawberry jam in those little containers at the bottom," she said. "Also a plastic knife."

"I figured."

"You're not even surprised."

"You got everything else right; it makes sense you'd get that."

"Then I don't see why—"

"No," Bender said. "I will not be your boyfriend. You can't do these things by logic."

"I already know that," Cindy said. "This has nothing to do with logic." She allowed him a few nibbles of the croissant and a sip of coffee in silence. "She broke your heart, didn't she, Bender?"

"Who broke my heart?"

"The woman who gave you the cat."

— ❧ —

Bender made kung pao chicken the evening Heather brought Taxi into his life and, later that same night, agreed to move in with him. He'd had no inkling of the events in store for him when he began preparing the meal, only that he was feeling expansive and adventurous and knew that Heather would be coming for dinner.

She brought the cat in a wicker transport which she set in the bedroom to give Taxi a chance to become accustomed to what she called the scents and humors of its new venue. Bender took a cautious peek at Taxi while Heather informed him that it was not uncommon for a cat to live for fifteen years. "That's a long time," he said, looking from the cat to her, hopeful there was some analogy forthcoming to their relationship as lovers. He would be fifty-three then. The thought of Heather then, enhanced by the road wear of life was so intense, his hand shook, spilling wine from his glass.

"What?" she said.

"I was thinking how you'd look then."

"And?"

"And I want it."

Taxi seemed content to remain in the wicker cat transport while Bender and Heather went at the kung pao chicken, which turned out to be all to the good, because halfway through the meal, Heather began toying with a peanut on her plate. In a matter of moments she threw the peanut at Bender. For a moment Bender was stunned. He was not used to being the sort of man women threw peanuts at. Such things happened to Wolfe all the time, it seemed.

Of course, Wolfe was dapper. English. Charming. Bender was able to stay neat, but doing so required effort. Unless he was using one of his "on" voices, the street twang of Oakland resided in his voice like a berry seed, stuck between his teeth. Forget charming; Bender was a teenager on a first date with a shirt that wouldn't stay tucked in and breath redolent of cinnamon chewing gum. He quickly recovered and reciprocated with a peanut from his own plate, initiating two of the most memorable hours in his life to date, during the course of which, among other things, Heather snuggled her head against his shoulder and told him, "You are a true loony, Bender, but I do think I could get used to you."

"You could start by moving your things over here. Then you could bring yourself." For a while, listening to her rhythmic breathing, Bender thought she might have fallen asleep without hearing him. A big jump from tossing a peanut to asking a woman to move in with you. Would he have the patience to wait until she woke up, and the courage to ask her again? When he turned toward her, he was rewarded by the sight of her nodding.

Bender knew enough not to overdo a good thing. First anniversary dinner was kung pao chicken, but he was careful not to cast the first peanut. Sometimes, when memorizing lines for a new play, he'd look up to watch her painting watercolors or playing with Taxi, wanting to honk toy horns or carve initials on tree trunks. Over a period of several weeks, he watched with fascination as Heather constructed and mounted on various of their walls shoe-box-sized condominiums for Taxi. "You will think of me every time you see him at play," she said.

A bit after the two-year mark, Bender began to notice Heather was no longer leaving notes in his shaving gear. One evening, she confronted him with a Styrofoam cup filled with rubber bands. "Is this what I think it is?"

Bender reddened. "Yes," he said. "I saved them."

"Jesus, Bender." A first; she'd called him Matt or Matthew before. "I suppose you saved every goddamned one."

Bender was also not the sort of person women shot rubber bands at. Love notes came in all forms, didn't they? Why wouldn't you want to save love notes?

"Yes," he said. "Every goddamned one."

Heather's prediction that Bender would think of her every time he saw Taxi proved as accurate as such things can be. At the same time, the prediction was as dramatic as Heather could be. Having a cat that was likely to endure until Bender was into his fifties, reminding him of Heather and the intensity of their relationship, was no easy thing. Nor had the intensity of their relationship been an easy thing. At about the same time, Bender came home from a rehearsal one afternoon and saw the U-Haul trailer attached to Heather's car, he'd already begun to wonder if it were possible to care so much for another person and still have enough of himself for work. Hadn't Wolfe gone through the same thing over Madeline, the trapeze artist, over just that matter?

"Too intense, Bender," Heather said, confronting him with a box of her clothes. She blew at a wisp of hair that had covered her eye. Bender gave her a solemn nod, took the box from her, and carried it to the trailer with the same sense of destiny he'd felt when carrying her things into his loft, or when the peanut bounced off his chest. It was in his mind to ask what was so bad about intensity and to point out the number of things in their respective orbits having nothing to do with intensity, things whose essential natures were blandness. But this sounded argumentative and defensive, the I-should-have-said spirit of the staircase carried forward to the spirit of the departing lover in a rented truck, and so he continued moving boxes.

"Even though you are a nut case," she told him, "I have gotten used to you and I love you very dearly, but we are frying my circuitry, Bender. I feel as though my nerves have split ends."

After Heather left, Taxi seemed satisfied with the life Bender gave it, but Heather had been right in her prediction: Taxi was an ongoing reminder of her. Taxi's presence added to the time it cost him to reach the point where he could begin to consider other women. It was bad enough that his attempts at intimacy with them evoked unsatisfactory comparisons with Heather, including the time he sat in a Chinese restaurant on Milpas Street, across from Janet, hefting a shelled peanut.

"What's that?" Janet said.

Bad enough. Having Taxi in his life seemed to be mocking him in a snide stage whisper.

— ❧ —

While taking his curtain calls for the final performance of *Twelfth Night,* Bender felt a stirring elation at the audience response. The clapping and clamor were more emphatic for his rendition of Feste than for Wolfe's Sebastian. Wolfe noticed it, too. "Friendship go hang," Wolfe muttered sotto voce while taking a bow. "From now on, you're competition and fair game for scene stealing. Girlfriends, too, come to think of it."

In his cubicle, toweling off the sweat and makeup, Bender felt the elation of good work turn bittersweet at the thought that Heather had not been there to see him. A postcard from her, addressed to him at the theater, had the plaintive cry of her own bewilderment: "Oh, Bender!" Nor would she be there to help decorate the new living quarters he'd be moving into. He felt a pang over the awareness that the cohesive unit of the cast, the play, and their combined, temporary possession of it and of each other was about to scatter. He would, of course, see Wolfe again, but he might not see some of the others in the cast again. The Big Bang, sending shards of the universe in all directions.

"So what about it, Bender?" Cindy, all legs and energy, still costumed as Viola, broke into his self-pity. "Be a sport. Take me to the cast party."

Bender could see the vulnerability in her posture, androgynous from her costume, projecting a bravery and insouciance she did not feel over the closing of the play and the impending loss of contact between them. What was the harm in a little kindness? His irritation with her infatuation would shift soon enough to amused tolerance. But her response showed him the potential for harm and mischief he already knew to be present. All traces of her androgyny were gone with his agreement to take her to the cast party. Bender felt a stirring for Cindy, and he turned away from her before she could read it in his face.

The party was being held at a sprawling home nestled into a hillside in the part of Santa Barbara called the Riviera. As he wound the Volvo up the sinuous streets, the altitude afforded them a view of the harbor and the busy movement of traffic heading north and south on 101. "You were good tonight, Bender," she said, resting her head on his shoulder. "Another week and you'd have been awesome."

The fact that Bender had thought this himself did not ease his discomfort with Cindy. She knew too much for someone her age.

"I'm going to miss you." Simple statement. There was weight but no pleading in her voice. She let it rest there, and, as they drove, her silence worked a tension on him. He found himself wanting her to push it just a bit more so that he could have some irritation to fall back on, should his resolve weaken. Seventeen. When Bender had been seventeen he hadn't at all been sure what he wanted. There was no way he could have done the equivalent to any role that Cindy had done as Viola in this production.

"Eighteen," Cindy said.

Bender took his eyes off the curve of the road to look at her. "You're reading my mind again," he said.

Her eyes were closed but there was a smile on her face. "Eyes on the road, Bender."

When they arrived at the party, Leah Cantwell, the hostess, drew him away from Cindy to introduce him to distinguished-looking middle-aged and elderly individuals, or couples who singled his performance out for praise. Bender caught sight of Wolfe across the room, also being passed from small group to small group like self-published books of vacation photos. Seeing this, Bender understood the *quid pro quo*. The cast got a better party than they could have arranged on their own, and Leah Cantwell got the edge with her friends for being a patron of the arts.

"I could introduce you to a number of influential people," Leah said, sleek, coifed, just the right amount of jewelry—a single rope of pearls and one fine-meshed tennis bracelet—to offset the plainness of her black sheath dress. He tried to imagine her snapping rubber bands.

Here it comes, Bender thought. Leah Cantwell looking to acquire an actor. As if on cue, she gave his forearm a squeeze. He wondered if she had similarly squeezed any portion of Wolfe's anatomy and, if so, how Wolfe had responded. Bender hooked a flute of champagne from a tray borne by a server from the great servant class of Santa Barbara, college students. He was about to raise the flute to his lips when a similar glass was clinked against his by Sanford Johns, his elegant dinner jacket taking the years away from his bent frame. "Why so glum, kid? You did a good job tonight."

"Closing-night blues," Bender told him. "I was just getting the groove of this play and this cast."

Johns shook his head. "Can't catch lightning in a bottle, kid. Drink up. Then get a new job. I just signed a three-book contract. Pretty good for a ninety-two-year-old, but given the alternative—" He extended his hand, then twisted it alternating palm up with palm down, the age old pantomime for either/or. "See what I mean?"

Bender saw all right. Heraclitus. You can't bathe in the same river twice. You can't be in the same role twice. You can't be lovesick the same way twice.

Several glasses of champagne later, Wolfe approached him, seeming as friends do, to have access to one another's thoughts. "Neither can you throw up the same canapé twice. But you'll come close if you keep drinking at your present pace."

Not bad for a new convert to AA. Wolfe didn't scold or preach, and Bender felt a wave of affection for him. It was true, Bender was on his way. Lit. Sloshed. Bagged. He liked the sound of all those words and the feelings of immunity they implied to the gloom about them.

"You could stay here," Leah Cantwell suggested at one point.

"He's already got plans," Cindy said, appearing at his side and looping her arm through his.

Bender watched with quiet amusement. Buoyed by Cindy's spunk, he watched older, richer, wiser Leah Cantwell allow her plucked—or was it woven— brow to arch. "Another time, then," she said.

Bender had it in mind to compliment Leah for the added quality of patience, and he thought to assure her not to worry; Cindy was too young for him, but his tongue was heavy, his mouth cottony, admittedly the pleasant cotton of Perrier-Jouet champagne, and the moment passed.

Cindy held out her hand. "Your keys, sport."

"You think I can't drive," Bender said.

"I know you can't."

"Ridiculous," Bender said.

152

He said it again as they wound down the corkscrew turns of Las Alturas Road, then asked Cindy to please drive slower, then to stop as the need came surging upon him to return some of the contents of his stomach to the cosmos without taking the time to digest them. A fit of giggling overcame him as he retched over a blue ceanothus shrub. Wolfe was wrong. It was possible to throw up the same canapé twice.

"Lay back, dear man," Cindy said when he returned to the car. "You're in good hands."

He believed her. Cindy was competent. There was no reason not to follow her instructions now. She seemed to understand the situation with a wisdom beyond her years when she told him to keep his eyes closed until they were on level ground again, and he was relieved not to have any symptoms of dizziness reaching to claim him.

Cindy's grasp of the situation was insightful; she had somehow secured a pleasant rinse wash to remove the acid taste from his mouth. Then they were parked somewhere, and, while Cindy removed his shoes, there was an interesting conversation in which Cindy spoke of something being obviated. *Obviate* was a lovely word; it pleased Bender that Cindy knew it. He lapsed comfortably into sleep with thoughts of how sensible and remarkable an emerging young woman Cindy was. Some man— aah! some men would be very fortunate.

— ♣ —

Not obviating, you fool. Obviating was wrong.

Bender woke with a throbbing awareness of a bad dream. A prompter, looking very much like Wolfe, was calling to Bender from the wings, script in hand, a frown of exasperation coming to life. The actor's nightmare. Being on stage and forgetting one's lines. But this was the actor's nightmare magnified. The prompter was telling Bender he not only had the wrong lines, he had the wrong play.

"Not obviating, you fool!"

When he sat up, he barely missed whacking his skull on the

153

inner roof header of the Volvo. Some pounding continued inside his head from last night's drinking, but thanks to the mouthwash, no oral uproar. What came to him first was the fact that he was not alone. Cindy lay not only next to him but entwined with him. Taxi had burrowed in next to Cindy.

Bender shook Cindy awake.

"Good morning, dear man," she said, departing from Bender's previous experiences in waking up women who slept next to him. There was no trace of crankiness about Cindy. Give her a few more years.

"What are you doing here, Cindy?"

"Very dear man," Cindy offered a mischievous smile.

"No," Bender said. "Tell me I'm wrong."

Cindy shook her head.

"Tell me I'm wrong, dammit."

Cindy propped herself up with an elbow and profiled toward him as Taxi yawned, then stretched.

"Ovulating," Bender said.

"I loved the part where you refused to use protection, then said you'd never felt so unthreatened by the prospect of parenthood." She nuzzled into his shoulder.

Bender smacked his forehead with his palm. Although pleased by the momentary effects of Cindy's burrowing gesture, he was, as well, torn by the implications of what had happened while his defenses were out on some cattle call. In a consummate misery, he lurched upward, this time bumping his head. Bender swore, then began casting around for his shoes.

Without pausing to let the engine of the Volvo warm up or to locate the shoes, he drove from their parking site beyond the Bird Refuge through the maze of streets that brought them to Von's shopping center in the Montecito Lower Village.

He led Cindy through the parking lot, uttering an involuntary yawp at the discovery that the drugstore had not yet opened. Still clutching her wrist, he moved them to a table in front of the Xanadu Coffee Shop. "Order some breakfast," he said.

Cindy was being much too pleased to suit him.

154

"I can't believe—" he started. But the truth was that he didn't know what it was of these circumstances that he didn't believe. Was it that he had no memory of the past night's events after Cindy had brought the car to rest in the place he'd been occupying these past weeks? What about the implications of the moral lapse of allowing himself to act on his lust? That would certainly help explain the faulty memory.

"I want you to know something," Cindy told him. "I was the aggressor, at least until—" She allowed her eyes to cast down toward her tented hands before she spoke. "Until you got with the program."

Bender could see a tinge of blush creep into her cheeks. "It was very special with you," she said. "The boys I actually messed around with before I knew you?" She shook her head. "Kinderspiel. Absolute child's play."

As the waitress took their order, Cindy reached across the table and squeezed his arm. "You've made me a very happy person, Bender."

His attention was pulled away from her by the sight of the pharmacist at the drugstore, opening the door for business and stopping to tie the waist strings of his smock. Bender rose, urged Cindy to her feet, and led her across the patio to the drugstore.

The pharmacist, a round, balding man with rimless glasses, smiled reassuringly, and Bender found himself wondering if there were any other profession that inspired such across-the-board confidence. "Pregnancy testing kit," Bender said. "Which are the most reliable?"

Reassurance transformed itself into a Norman Rockwell archetype as the pharmacist moved to a shelf just beyond contraceptives and personal lubricants. "We stock Fact Plus, ep, Inverness. They're all pretty much the same in function and price," he said. "Each requires some urine from the mother-to-be. But this—" He lifted a green-and-white box, extending it toward Bender. "—is the one I get the most calls for. First Response." He nodded approval. "Supposedly quite reliable. And let me say how refreshing it is to see a father take such an interest in his daughter's venture into motherhood."

"He's not—"

"She's not—"

Bender and Cindy spoke at once, exchanged glances when they recognized the phenomenon, then gave it a final emphasis by stopping at the same moment.

The pharmacist took in this synchronicity with a pinched frown. "Beast," he hissed at Bender. "How could you?"

Cindy put a finger to her lips. "You shouldn't blame him," she said. "He really tried not to."

Bender had her by the elbow. "Come on," he said. "We're getting you to a rest room." To the pharmacist he said, "We'll take a First Response and an Inverness."

"Beast," the pharmacist told him.

— ♣ —

"You're sure you don't want to go for threesies?" Cindy regarded him over the remains of their breakfast dishes with a cheeriness that gnawed at him. "We could try one of the other kits."

Bender shook his head, watching her consider an uneaten piece of his toast, opt in its favor, then begin to spread it with the remains of his marmalade. There was a lesson to be learned here, but he was not at all sure what it was. Cindy was bright, street smart beyond her years, imbued with an appetite for life. He felt a profound regret at not being able to recall any of the activities they'd indulged in in the back of the Volvo last night. If she were indeed pregnant as a result of it, there was no doubt in his mind what would have to be done, and that would be a problem, too. Landing sites in his conscience were already ticking with plans and contingencies, tempting him, mocking him.

"What was her name, Bender?" Cindy asked, sweeping crumbs from her chin. "The lady who gave you Taxi?"

Having already gone so far as to visualize this potential offspring of his and Cindy's, Bender went on to visualize it first as boy then girl. He found himself not caring which. Either would do. From that uneasy epiphany, he went on to seeing himself

156

diapering the child while Cindy looked on with approval. As if these were not enough, he went on to see himself without the slightest bitterness at having this hostage to fortune—these two hostages really. Bender now suffered a sharp pang of guilt at her question. "Heather," he said. "Her name is Heather." As in, Oh Bender!

"Took your mind off her at least for a while, didn't I?"

Bender found this unanswerable. After he was silent for a while, Cindy usurped the last piece of his toast. She took a large chomp out of it, seeming to enjoy it and the situation. "The thing is, Bender," she observed between chews, "you'll get over Heather, but you'll always remember me."

— ❧ —

Bender had the feeling he was being watched, a feeling that had been recurring for the past two or three days and which was now heightened to a laser-like intensity. Sitting in the sumptuous, light-drenched patio of the Arts and Letters Cafe, conscious of how fashionable Leah Cantwell looked in her silk paisley dress and single rope of cultured pearls, Bender let his eyes take in the other tables in the courtyard, thinking to catch his watcher by surprise.

When his surveillance was completed, he was none the wiser. There were, of course, no clues, no one he recognized in the amiable setting of individuals, some of them as well dressed as Leah Cantwell, chattering, laughing, gesturing over lunch. He tried to tell himself that his sense of being under scrutiny was the consequence of his conscience nagging him for having accepted this date with Leah Cantwell.

He indulged the exercise given him by his mentor shortly before her death. "No setting is neutral to an actor, Matthew. Whenever you are in a place, no matter where it is, look for a word that describes its effect on you. Are you frightened? Secure? Comfortable?

"Watched," Bender told her ghost.

"To your new living accommodations," Leah Cantwell

toasted him with a glass of flinty, chilled Chardonnay. "And to the Santa Barbara Police Department for putting it within your reach."

Bender was waiting for the other shoe to drop, some reference to her agenda for pursuing him. Leah Cantwell, although elegant, pleasing to look at, and capable of substantial conversation, was beyond suitability for him as anything other than a toy. Clinking his own glass of wine against hers, he bought time from the complexities of his failed relationship with Heather. Intensity, the very thing that had doomed him and Heather, was missing in any image of himself and Leah Cantwell. Was that the secret of power? No intensity, no potential for pain.

"You're probably wondering—" Leah Cantwell's smile featured dentistry every bit as elegant as her rope of pearls. "You're probably wondering why l asked you here today."

Bender liked her directness to the point of feeling a stirring his loins, but he wanted none of the game. "I have no doubt at all."

Her response was cut short by the arrival of a waitress pushing a food trolley. The waitress, tall, starkly angular, with dramatic piles of gray hair and a jowly set to her jaw, spoke in an accent Bender couldn't quite place at first. "Well," she said, "here we are then. The soup course." She set a large bowl before Leah Cantwell, who immediately wrinkled her nose, then began shaking her head.

"I didn't order soup," Leah Cantwell said.

"Course you did," the waitress told her, referencing a check. "Says right here. You ordered the split pea."

Bender's turn came next as the waitress set a large tureen before him, and then lifted the lid to allow a savory waft of steam. "Mulligatawny," the waitress said. "Right nice choice there, too."

"Wrong table," Bender said. "I didn't order mulligatawny. I ordered the Reuben sandwich."

"Ah, I get it," the waitress said, tapping the check. "Had a few glasses of Chardonnay and changed our minds, did we? Getting on too tiddily and want something more substantial."

"This is impossible," Leah Cantwell said. "Neither of us ordered soup. You have the wrong table."

"Wrong table is it?" The waitress said, her voice rising in timbre. She thrust the check at Bender. "What's it say here under table number?"

Bender squinted at some cramped handwriting. "Table A-6," he read.

The waitress made a flourish of lifting a condiment pot, which she extended to Bender. "What's it say on the bottom?"

"It says Table A-6. But that has nothing to do with—"

"I don't care what it says," Leah Cantwell stormed. "I did not order soup."

"All right then," the waitress said, sweeping up the bowl in front of Leah. "Have it your way."

"Careful," Bender warned, but it was too late. A trail of soup flew from the bowl and splattered at the elegant shoulders of Leah Cantwell's dress.

"That was certainly clumsy," Leah said, jumping to her feet. Bender poked his napkin into his drinking water and began dabbing at the offending stain, radiating a gelatinous path toward her bosom, but Leah pushed his hand away. "You're not making it any better. If you can't be constructive, at least stay out of the way." She gave him an icy glare, looked about the room, and started toward the lobby.

"Wrong way, luv," the waitress said. "Loo's over there." She pointed toward a side alcove. When Leah Cantwell had made sufficient progress, the waitress turned to Bender. "Some temper, huh, sport? Better to find out now, before things get sticky." Bender became aware of the maitre d' advancing on them across the courtyard with grim purpose. His own attempts at seriousness were useless. "All right," Bender asked Cindy. "How did you do it?"

Cindy had already removed rolls of cotton from her mouth. She swept the large, gray wig from her head and gave a low curtsy. "Not 'how,' sport. That was a piece of cake." Cindy rubbed her nose with the back of her hand. "The question you should be asking is 'Why?'"

At which point the maitre d' arrived and took Cindy by the arm. "I'll have an explanation for this behavior," he said.

Bender was having explanations of his own. "We didn't really have sex, did we? That was a Cindy performance—just like this one."

"You'll always wonder, Bender," she said. She acknowledged the maitre d' with a courtly bow. "Explanation?" She asked him. "You want an explanation? All right," she said. "Love. I did it for love."

"I don't think," the maitre d' said, drawing her away from the table and toward the exit, "your love and my clientele go together."

"You'll always wonder, Bender," Cindy called. He watched her grand exit as she was led through tables of curious diners, a considerable scattering of applause already echoing off the patio walls.

For some intangible future, Bender had living arrangements beyond the Volvo that included a modest stipend for services as a night watchman. He had a notional cat, an ex-lover who sometimes sent him postcards that simply read, "Oh, Bender!" and an acting job, albeit a freebie, for the benefit of the Santa Barbara Police Department.

"Now what?" Bender asked the Cosmos as the applause began to fade.

Coming to Terms

When the invitation came this year, Charlie Citron's first thought was to decline, then face the repercussion, rather than appear and take those consequences.

Past announcements of his department chairman's reception triggered only mild distaste, the foreboding of a few hours of boredom or, if things did become oppressive, a morning-after hangover from too much of the sweet sherry Norman Brandenberg purchased in bulk from a family outside Solvang.

But for some time now, Charlie had been suffering reversals. Contentious students seemed drawn to his classes. His essay "Alienation and Anomie in the Urban Landscape," scheduled as the lead piece in a prestigious refereed journal, was returned to him when the editor resigned over some political principle. In spite of his best efforts to feed his cat a healthy diet, Sanders was afflicted with urinary tract problems. Jillian, his recent venture with romance, which looked so promising at the onset, ended in flaming disaster.

Charlie began to slog about as though his soul wore a hair shirt. Vulnerable, flinching at the merest confrontation, his viscera would wrench up on him at the sight of borrowed books, notes and correspondence, concert ticket stubs, or any trace of the confetti of his failed relationship.

At one low point, the discovery in his laundry hamper of a single white athletic sock belonging to the departed Jillian caused Charlie such a pang that he dropped to his haunches, then leaned his forehead against the molding of the bathroom door frame to await the impending arrival of tears.

The thought of suffering through Brandenberg's reception was more than Charlie could bear, but talk about reversals, Charlie's strategy to make himself scarce from it was dealt the blow of an accidental encounter with Norman Brandenberg himself, one afternoon in the faculty lounge. "Ah, Citron," he said. "There you are." Even in a simple greeting Brandenberg had the capacity to sound accusatory. A short man who often wore suits with large patterns, his speech cadences were reminiscent of an exercise instructor. "Should have known I'd find you in the lounge. Who are you bringing to the reception?"

Charlie's timing was off. The opportunity to defect lost a critical beat of momentum. "The truth is—" he began.

"You haven't asked anyone yet. Excellent." Brandenberg shot his shirt cuffs. "You can bring that poet no one seems to understand. Marlys."

"Jesus, Norman," Charlie said.

Brandenberg tilted his head back, a gesture Charlie knew to be the result of the man's ongoing fear of jowl sag. "Vague her poetry may be, Citron, but those other rumors about her have no foundation." He reflected on this for a moment, appeared to satisfy himself, then nodded. "Very well. Marlys, it is. And Citron? We need to talk. Soon."

Charlie knew what that was all about. He was beset by visions of confrontational students, waving exam blue books in his face, challenging the curriculum, demanding grade changes. "My new course, right? The Absurdist Novel."

"Afraid," Brandenberg grimaced, "it goes beyond a single course."

"All right," Charlie steeled himself, "let's have it."

Brandenberg wore a watch with a large dial, a calibrated bezel, and a number of other functions to measure actual time and elapsed time. "Can't," he said, checking its face. "Already behind schedule, thanks to looking for you. We'll talk Saturday. Don't forget Marlys."

The necessary telephone transactions involving arrangements to escort Marlys to Brandenberg's reception were rendered disastrous when Marlys mistook Charlie for a bookstore manager who had made unwanted sexual gestures at her recent poetry reading. To compound the matter, Charlie was over an hour late, thanks to his getting lost as he tried to find Marlys's cottage in an ecologically-sensitive new development off the Cathedral Oaks area of Santa Barbara, where street signs were considered an outrage.

After leaving Marlys clustered by a group of her students in the Brandenberg living room, Charlie braved the buffet, which proved to be yet another disaster. Aware of the growing impatience of those behind him in the serving line, he felt himself losing ground in his struggle with a link of kielbasa that refused to detach itself from the large coil in the chafing dish.

All he wanted now was to cut his losses, to extricate his fork from this culinary tar baby, then move on to something safer, say the stuffed cabbage rolls. In spite of his determination and focus on his task, he became aware of a man with sharp facial planes, aviator-style glasses, and thick, crinkly hair pointing at him.

"You, there," the man said.

"Are you talking to me?" Charlie continued wrestling with his fork.

"Film noir, right?"

"Excuse me?"

"You're the film noir. Mitchum. Dick Powell. John Ireland. And those pouty, moist-lipped women." The man advanced, extending a hand. "I'm the *bildungsroman*. Just came on board." With a hitch of his head, he surveyed the room. "Some gathering, isn't it? I understand Norman does this every year."

Charlie was spared having to answer by the appearance of the host, wearing a horse-blanket plaid jacket accented by a paisley ascot. "Ah," he said. "I see you've met." He took charge of Charlie's elbow. "You can catch up with Simmons later, Citron," he said. "We've got to have our chat. As soon as you decide how much sausage you mean to take."

Norman Brandenberg steered Charlie past the living room, through a group of thoughtful listeners who seemed to be nodding in cadence to Marlys as she read from her new poetry chapbook. "Aggressive fellow, that Simmons." Brandenberg spoke sotto voce. "Had an eye out for one of your classes." Brandenberg lowered his voice further, introducing a note of incredulity. "Wanted to do his own spin on the film noir. Something Jungian, if you can believe it. 'Shadows, Archetypes, and Shady Women.' The mind recoils at the thought. But I was firm on your proprietary rights. Told him you had seniority and the credentials."

While Charlie debated asking why Simmons had been hired in the first place, his attention was drawn to the edge of the group listening to Marlys read. He soon saw the reason why: a leggy woman with sunburned cheeks and ropy red hair that tumbled down her back like an eloper's ladder. The crinkles in her face and the amusement they spoke toward Marlys's performance captured Charlie and, in less than a moment, broke his heart.

Passing at close enough range to get the color of the woman's eyes, Charlie felt himself energized by the sight of her. But a penumbra clouded his psyche. How did one go about attracting such a woman? She was at least two inches taller than he. She radiated waves of assurance and poise. He had thinning hair, two cowlicks, and a moustache that came in red on one side, giving the impression of a jam stain on his lip unless he shaved twice a day. With such whimsical trappings, how did you get such vibrant enlightened cynicism as this woman to become a part of your life? "The film noir," he said, "is not my class. I took it for one meeting when Hazeltine's back went out."

They arrived at the door to the study, where Brandenberg held the door open for Charlie to enter. "My classes are all related to the novel, Norman. The Nineteenth-Century Novel. The Twentieth Century American. The Twentieth Century British."

"Your classes. Exactly what I wanted to talk to you about."

164

Directing Charlie to a chair, Brandenberg perched on the edge of his Queen Anne desk. "We do have a problem with your classes."

"This new batch of students," Charlie chose his words with care. "They're very conservative. They take everything so literally. Even the Nineteenth Century Novel of Protest upsets them. They think Dickens was overreacting."

"This isn't about politics, Citron. This is something else entirely. Of all the faculty in our department," he paused, "you have the highest incidence of students experiencing emotional breakdowns."

— ❧ —

By the time the first member of the group finished his presentation, Charlie was starting to fidget. He caught himself once again, checking to see if his socks matched. He was one of about fifteen people in a large room insulated with discolored sound-proofing squares, some of which seemed to hang from the wall like Post-It notes on a refrigerator. Judging from the number of floor-mounted electrical outlets, telephone conduits, and the uneven wear pattern on the discolored institutional carpeting, the room could very well have served as clerical office space for an insurance company or other large institution. A number of tomb-like vending machines at one side of the room dispensed coffee and snacks. The group sat in uncomfortable institutional chairs deployed in an attenuated circle about the facilitator, a prematurely graying woman in her early forties who wore a business suit, pink athletic socks, and running shoes.

From somewhere in the room, Charlie detected the distracting scent of chicken soup. The next speaker added more momentum to his sensation of discomfort. When the third speaker began listing her strategies for overcoming bulimia binges, Charlie had the same trapped feeling he sometimes experienced at Norman Brandenberg's receptions.

At the break, when some of the group members went out on the fire escape to smoke, buy coffee or snacks from the vending machines, or simply visit, Charlie approached the facilitator, whose name tag identified her as Ginger. "I'm afraid this isn't working for me," he told her.

"Suit yourself," she intoned. "Go ahead, bail out now. But I can't give you credit for the full meeting, and that means you've violated the conditions of your parole. They'll have your ass back in front of the judge so fast your head will swim."

Charlie found himself shaking his head involuntarily. "You don't understand."

"Oh, right," Ginger persisted. "You're not really an alcoholic. You've just had a run of bad luck."

"As a matter of fact," Charlie ventured, "you're correct on both counts."

"Get real, Cook." Ginger prodded his chest. "How many DUI's does it take to convince you? Screw up this time, your driver's license is history."

Charlie shook his head again. Ginger began flipping the pages on her clip board. "You're not Steven Harvey Cook?" She ran a thumbnail down the last page. "I thought you were a blue card. Excuse me. That's bureaucratese for a court-order person. Probationary compliance people have blue authorization folders. You're a pink card; that means insurance. Why didn't you say something, Citron? Am I pronouncing it right? Why didn't you speak up, Charlie?"

"Things haven't been going well all year," Charlie said. "My department chairman thinks I'm driving my students over the edge and he wants me to find out why."

"Generalities won't cut it, Charlie. We don't have much time. Your insurance covers—" She consulted his pink folder, "—six sessions. Six sessions to get you back on your feet, Charlie." Now Ginger appeared to be drawn by something behind him, looking over his shoulder, giving Charlie the distinct impression she was losing interest. "If," she said, turning her face back to him, "if I'm to be any help, you've got to give me something to go on. Do you understand?"

"Jillian," Charlie said. "She walked out on me."

"Don't hold back on me, Charlie. Six sessions can go pretty fast, and there's no more funding for the current symptom."

166

Once again, Charlie felt Ginger's attention begin to drift to a point over his shoulder. In spite of himself, he raised his voice. "She accused me of being enigmatic, impenetrable."

"Were you?"

Charlie's temper was continuing to flare. She could at least look at him. "I suppose," he said, "I might have seemed that way. I was worried about Sanders."

"You mean you were jealous that she might care more about this Sanders fellow than you."

Charlie saw his control of everything sneaking out of the room. Ginger wasn't even looking at him, and she appeared to be counting to herself. He was sure he saw her sub-vocalizing a three and then a four. Against all his efforts, Charlie began to cry, the sobs causing his words to slur. "Sanders is my cat, god-dammit, and he has urinary tract troubles, and you aren't even goddamn listening."

"Six. Seven," Ginger said. "I heard everything you said, but you've got to help me. Come on." She was moving across the room in quick strides toward the vending machines where the third speaker, a spindly woman in a sheath dress, stood off to one side, trying to appear nonchalant by gazing at a framed watercolor of a desert sunset.

"Will you come on," Ginger called to Charlie, advancing on the woman in the sheath dress, pinning her against the wall, and beginning to shake her.

By the time Charlie arrived, a crowd had assembled. Ginger continued to shake the other woman, who was beginning to whimper. At first Charlie was baffled by what he saw at her feet, then he recognized the unique packaging of Hostess Twinkies.

"Five," Ginger said, still shaking her quarry until another pack of Twinkies fell to the floor. "That's six. I saw you buy seven from that machine. Going to have yourself a binge, were you?"

Charlie saw the seventh pack of Twinkies tucked between the woman's arm and her upper torso. Approaching her, he lifted her arm, took the package of Twinkies from her, then handed it to Ginger.

To Charlie's fascination, Ginger put one arm around the bulimic woman, wrapping her in a comforting hug. "You don't need to do this, Angela," she smoothed. "I don't know why you do it, but you don't have to."

The bulimic woman began to sob. From this, Charlie and a number of the others understood that some crisis had passed.

Starting back to the circle of chairs where the group was held, Charlie's eyes fastened on the gaze of Ginger. "I heard everything you said, Citron," she told him. "Your cat was in pain, and it scared the hell out of you because you felt helpless, and it represented everything in your life that you couldn't control."

— ❧ —

"All right, everyone." Ginger peered around the group. "What does Charlie need?" This was his third venture at what Ginger liked to call an encounter session. The classic enormity of the problems, legal, psychical, and moral, of the other members had begun to impress Charlie. Substance abuse. Violent natures. Illegal trafficking in contraband. Armed robbery. Wasn't there a kind of electrifying excitement inherent in having such individuals review his travails and suggest strategies for him? Like having Bonnie and Clyde on your faculty review team. Norman Brandenberg could scarcely have visualized such colleagues for him when he directed Charlie to use his faculty insurance policy for the psychological need option.

A stocky man with steel-frame glasses, known to be prison issue, a pencil-thin moustache, and enormous pectorals stood to be recognized. "What Charlie needs," he said, "is to get laid."

"You may be right, Dominick," Ginger nodded, "but no fair using that as your solution to every problem."

"Hey, right is right," ventured Wanda, a housewife who sold sexual favors to support a substance habit. "A little nookie wouldn't hurt him none. Take some of the edge off, right Charlie?" Her piercing gaze held him, caused the back of his neck to itch.

"No soliciting in group, Wanda," this admonition from Ginger.

"A better haircut," called a broad-shouldered young woman who wore motorcycle boots and had a small butterfly tattooed on her left bicep. "His sideburns run too low."

"Come on," Ginger urged her. "Charlie doesn't have many hours left on his insurance. Let's give him some real help."

"I don't like the way he stands," a dapper little man in a double-breasted suit called out. "Not enough spunk."

"What the hell?" Charlie said. "Haircut? Posture? That's it?" Ginger waved him off. "We're starting to get a pattern here, Charlie. Who sees where this is going?"

An overweight blonde who wore gray sweat pants and carried a skate board raised her hand. When Ginger nodded, she said "Image."

"Very good, Loretta. Anything more?"

"Yeah," Loretta said. "Esteem."

"Bingo," Ginger said.

"I'm telling you. He gets laid, he gets all the esteem he needs."

"Esteem, Charlie," Ginger nodded. "Think about it while we take a short break."

Charlie loosened his tie. He was about to indulge himself with an apple from the vending machine when his attention was wrenched toward his left. Framed in the doorway, self-conscious and bewildered, was the tall red-haired woman he'd last seen in Norman Brandenberg's living room the day of his open house.

Charlie Citron, professor of modern literature, given citations by academic committees because of his keen grasp of existential issues, published in refereed journals for seeing things in such works as *Adam Bede, The Mill On the Floss,* and *The Vicar of Wakefield* that none of his brother or sister academics had seen before, that very Charlie Citron who inveighed against the use of the pathetic fallacy in student papers, was stunned by the vision of her to the point where his loins cried out to him. In mitigation, the Charlie Citron who was cohort and confidante of DUIs, burglars, depressives, and one individual who haunted laundromats in upscale shopping centers for the purpose of making off with select items of lingerie, that same Charlie Citron was suffused with urgent desire.

"Esteem, Charlie," Loretta clapped him on the back *en passant* to the soft drink cooler.

"Nookie," Dominick chided on his way to the fire escape for a smoke. "You get it, you'll see what I mean."

The red-haired woman was introduced to the group after break. "Hello, Bianca," they called out in unison after Ginger presented her and asked her to stand.

Charlie savored the knowledge of her name as though it were some greater key to understanding her. Caught up in the skeptical wisdom he'd acquired in the past three weeks, he almost missed an important discovery: Bianca's folder was blue. She was more than a pink-folder occupational stress-out like him. She was bigger fish. She'd reached some legal breaking point, had been in a court where a judge decided enough was enough—either therapy or the slammer. Bianca had yet to speak a word as a group member, and still Charlie had this intimate knowledge of her, which caused his pulse to quicken from the excitement.

"Now, where were we?" Ginger asked.

"Me," Charlie volunteered. "Me and my esteem." He allowed his focus to move to the point across the circle from him where Bianca sat, trying to achieve some comfort for her long body on the skimpy institutional chair. Her first response when she became aware of him was a non-committal smile, which was quickly replaced by what Charlie called the Look of Anomaly, a recognition of someone in an out-of-context situation.

"What about your esteem, Charlie?" Ginger bored in.

"Needs some touch-up work," Charlie acknowledged.

"Kick some ass, Charlie," a voice from the group urged.

"What about it?" Ginger said, consulting her notes. "A little show-down with your department chairman? Want to do a psychodrama and have someone portray Norman Brandenberg?"

"Tempting," Charlie said, aware of the involuntary gasp from Bianca when Norman Brandenberg's name was mentioned. "But I don't think that's the real issue."

"Bravo, Charlie," Ginger said. "You call the shot. Where do we go from here?"

Charlie smiled as he became aware of the recognition on

Bianca's face. Now she knew beyond a doubt where she'd seen him before. Once again she did something involuntarily; her hand covered her mouth.

— ❧ —

Bianca was the last member of the group to talk about her condition, starting just before the ten o'clock cut-off time. Charlie listened with the care he'd give a Victorian novel. Most of the blue-card people began with a straightforward account of how they came to their troubles with the law. The rest, notably the DUI people, were still in denial, complaining they were innocent or victims of police entrapment.

Bianca stood when she spoke, following the pattern of most of the more experienced blue-card people, causing Charlie to lean forward in his eagerness to hear of her infractions, "I'm here tonight," she said, "because of my inability to cope."

This announcement was greeted by hoots and catcalls from a number of the group members.

"Come on, Sweetie," Ginger urged. "Cut to the chase."

"I get into a good deal of trouble," Bianca said with a rush of breath, "because of men."

In spite of another round of hoots, Charlie experienced a surge of anticipation at this information. He broke ranks from the scoffers by urging Bianca to continue. "Tell us about it," he said. "All of it."

"In a nutshell," Ginger challenged.

"Nutshell it is," Bianca said, her eyes meeting Charlie's for a moment, then focusing on a point above and beyond him. "I am doomed," she spoke with a sharp intake of breath. "Men predictably find me attractive and desirable to the point where I despair of ever having a real relationship."

In the resulting pandemonium, Ginger adjourned the group.

— ❧ —

Charlie caught up with Bianca in the parking lot, thanks to

the stork-like pace her high heels forced upon her over the uneven asphalt paving. She struggled to fit her keys in the door of her Honda, but when she saw she had lost the race, she turned to face him full on. "I suppose," she said, "this will be all over campus tomorrow."

"Don't you think you're being a bit dramatic?"

Bianca fumbled in her purse. She found a pack of cigarettes and set about shaking one out, lighting it, then producing a defiant plume of smoke. "All right, let's hear the lecture. I shouldn't be smoking, right? An intelligent, educated person should know better, right? Therefore, I must be bent on self-destruction, and you, altruist and good Samaritan that you are, only came out here to offer me support."

"I followed you for a completely different purpose," Charlie said. "I wanted to see if you'd consider going out with me."

She took another pull on her cigarette, regarded it with distaste, then ground it into the asphalt with slow deliberation, her eyes on Charlie all the while. "Because you haven't been able to get me out of your mind since you last saw me."

Charlie shook his head. "I tried very hard not to think of you at all. How could I hope to attract you?"

"But now, you horny little worm, you've got the goods on me, and I have to go out with you, is that how you see it? I heard what they were saying about you in there. You even look desperate."

"By God," Charlie said, hoping to keep things on a serious plane but grinning in spite of himself, "you really *are* dramatic, aren't you?"

"Why else would I go out with you, Charlie Citron?"

The Charlie Citron who saw the unusual in *Adam Bede, The Mill on the Floss,* and *The Vicar of Wakefield* had some agreeable things to offer in his defense, but the Charlie Citron who was veteran of four grueling group therapy sessions could now put himself in the position of a doubter, a cynic, particularly a blue-card cynic. What a hash she would make of his romantic agenda.

Charlie gave in to inspiration. He took a cigarette from her, drew on it, blew a plume of smoke at her, then ground the cigarette on the pavement. "Because," he said, "you have no choice."

Bianca processed this information with a stoic nod. "Nothing like a reality check, is there?" She reached into her purse for her checkbook and handed Charlie a deposit slip with her address and phone number printed on it. "We can start with dinner tomorrow. I suppose you'll want to show me off all over town."

"Dinner tomorrow is fine," Charlie said, beginning to relish his illicit power, "but at your place."

Again the dispassionate nod. "Go ahead, gloat. You'll get your pound of flesh, Charlie Citron, but you'll get more than you bargained for." Her lips curled slightly. "For one thing, I'm a terrible cook. For another, I'm way too much woman for you. I'll fry your circuits. I'll melt your fuses." Her eyes fixed him. "You have no idea what you've got yourself into."

— ❧ —

Because he had leveraged his way into Bianca's life, her kitchen, and very possibly her bedroom by subterfuge, Charlie felt the moral imperative to bring a distinguished wine on his first visit. He chose the Wine Cask on Anacapa Street as his purchase point, where he was rewarded with the need for a three-block walk to find a parking space.

Only moments out of his car, his mind cluttered with choices between merlot, cabernet, and pinot, his imagination charging forth with visions of the lanky presence and provocative nature of his date, Charlie did not know what to make of the massive figure that appeared beside him. The sudden presence delivered a ham-fisted prod, driving Charlie off stride, sending him skittering to retain balance.

Another shove drove Charlie into a fence of eugina shrubs, through it and, ultimately, down on his hands and knees, with the realiziation that he was being mugged.

"I won't hurt you," a cold voice said, "unless I have to. You clear on that?"

When Charlie tried to respond, only a gurgle emerged, in consequence of which he bobbed his head.

"Where's your wallet?"

"Bub-breast pup-pocket," Charlie said, feeling further incapacitated by the extent of his jittery fear. A heavy force, hand or foot, pinned his right shoulder while a deft hand probed the pocket of his jacket, withdrew his breastfold.

Charlie's helplessness and vulnerability were beginning to congeal into a surge of anger. Foolish as it might have been to do so, he wanted to inflict some fear and surprise of his own on his attacker, but as quickly as it had begun, his revenge strategy came to an end with a drawn-out sound trumpeting above him. "Aw, sheet goddamn." Charlie's wallet thumped in the dust before him, flung with some force. Now Charlie felt himself being hoisted to his feet. "What the hell you doing in this neighborhood? Don't you know anything?"

On his feet now, Charlie suffered enormous hands dusting his shoulders and back. Turning to face his mugger, he confronted a tall slab of a man in dark corduroy trousers and a safari jacket, his large bony head shaking with disgust.

"Amos?" Charlie said, recognition beginning to dawn.

"Shee-it," the mugger said. "Amos is right. You in my Thursday group. How'm I supposed to rob you?"

Amos began to reflect solicitude to the point of more dusting of grass and eugina leaves from Charlie's trousers, inspecting Charlie's knees for any sign of tear, then reaching for Charlie's head, turning it as though inspecting a bowling ball for heft. "You need some witch hazel for that chin, you hear me?"

"I have some shaving lotion in the car," Charlie said. "That ought to do it."

The concept seemed to stun Amos. "What you got shaving lotion in the car for?"

"I have a date. I was on my way to get some wine."

"The tall drink of water? Red hair?"

Charlie felt himself begin to redden.

"Outstanding." Amos probed the depths of his pocket and emerged with a money-clipped sheaf of bills. From its considerable thickness, he pulled off two twenties. "Get Buttonwood 1993 Merlot," he instructed, proffering the bills. "Steep, but worth every cent. My treat." He appeared to reflect for a moment. "Best we keep this between ourselves, you know? Ginger, she find out you dating someone from the group, she have your ass."

— ❧ —

Bianca met him at the door wearing a terry-cloth robe and high-heeled mules, trailing behind her the unmistakable smoke and acrid tang of burning food. Her expression of resigned irritation gave way to open bitterness as she surveyed him. "Do you always show up for dates looking like you've just been mugged?"

Charlie shoved two bottles of wine at her. "Can we open one of these and have something to drink? Then I think we ought to talk."

"Oh, right," Bianca said. "Sure. Get acquainted. Seek the essential humanity in each other. As though we don't know why you're here."

Charlie thought he saw a momentary lowering of the guard when she looked at the labels on the wine bottles. "Why I'm here," he conceded. "That's what I want to talk about."

While she was in the kitchen, he moved about the small, comfortable living room where unfinished book cases took up all the available wall space. A large chintz sofa and a chintz-covered reading chair provided the only possibilities for seating. Scanning the shelves. Charlie quickly determined her interest was nineteenth- and early twentieth- century American authors.

Before he could find any other revealing facets of her personality, Bianca returned with an opened bottle and two glasses in time to catch him nodding approval. "You think you've found some key to my psyche, is that it? I have copies of *Sister Carrie* and *Jenny Gerhardt,* so you think there's symbolism."

Charlie took both glasses from her, poured a generous dollop in each, offered her one before he took a long pull on his. "They'll laugh at me in group for this if they find out," he shrugged. "And maybe they'll be right to laugh, but I can't go through with it." He drained his glass, couldn't find a place to set it down, then handed it to her. "Maybe it was being mugged, maybe it was finding you as attractive as I do. Either way, there's nothing like sudden vulnerability to make you realize how easy it is for power to backfire." He took the glass and the wine bottle back from her, poured himself another splash, then drained it. "It was very tempting. I almost think I could have gone through with it, but thanks all the same."

"I made dinner," Bianca said.

"We can keep this between ourselves. No one at group has to know and certainly no one on campus will hear about any of it—including your troubles with the law—from me."

"I cooked for you, goddammit. I made a flank steak and Brussels sprouts and there's Paul Newman's all-natural salad dressing."

"You are very attractive and intriguing." Charlie closed his eyes for a moment, then started to the door.

"You little creep, are you telling me you're passing up a sure thing because you like me?"

"That is very much the case," Charlie sighed and continued his retreat.

"How do you know you like me? You don't know anything about me," she called after him.

At the door, Charlie turned, feeling a tingling of pleasure within himself. "You like nineteenth- and twentieth-century American authors." Bianca made an inchoate croaking sound, greatly reminding him of his attempts to speak during his recent altercation with Amos. Charlie nodded in sympathy then closed the door behind him. Moments later, as he made his way down the pathway at the side of her apartment, Charlie heard Bianca call after him. "Do you have any idea what a turn on this is?" Charlie turned to regard her, standing just outside her front door. "I have burned the hell out of dinner, Charlie Citron, but I promise you'll enjoy dessert."

— ❧ —

After about fifteen minutes of sliding in and out of a comfortable doze, Charlie felt Bianca stir next to him, shifting position so that in the darkness he was aware of her turning on her side to face him. When she asked, "That's it?" the heat of her breath tickled his bare chest.

"I'm afraid so," he said, "Unless—"

"Aha, here it comes."

"Unless there's something I'm neglecting."

Bianca sighed in the darkness. "I'm talking about *you*. You don't want to tie me up or handcuff me to the bed or have me wear a nurse's uniform?"

"A sad reflection on my sophistication, I guess," Charlie conceded, "but I wouldn't begin to know what to do next if we got into any of that stuff."

Bianca reached past him to the night table, found her cigarettes, and lit up. In the brief flare of the lighter, her face was printed on his senses. "Then you're really through? Satisfied?"

"It's been a long time," Charlie said, "since I've been so comfortable. If I've left you wanting—"

"Never mind the gallantry," she said. "I manage quite well, thank you."

After a painful interval in which Charlie could hear the minutiae of household sounds—floors creaking, squirrels skittering about the roof outside, the asthmatic chuff and chug of plumbing sounds, the manic whirr of a refrigerator—and the purposeful breathing of Bianca, he had the sense of disorientation. Things were getting away from him, and he didn't know if he'd done something to disturb Bianca much less if his sin were one of omission or commission.

At length Bianca spoke. "You haven't a clue one about what's going on, have you?" She reached across him to mash her cigarette in the nightstand ashtray.

Even in the darkness, Charlie closed his eyes, prepared for the worst. "You find me enigmatic, impenetrable." He took a deep breath. "Boring."

"Don't say that," Bianca pleaded, grasping his shoulders and shaking him before she lay her head on his chest. "You have a streak of kindness I'm totally unused to. You aren't an enigma, you're almost transparent."

"If it's all the same to you," Charlie sighed, "I'd rather be enigmatic."

Bianca began shaking him again. "Don't you see what's happening? I'm drawn to you, Charlie Citron." She sat, reached across him to turn on the lamp. While Charlie's eyes were growing accustomed to the sting of sudden light, Bianca had reached for her cigarette lighter. "Here," she said, handing it to him. "I want you to have this."

"Thank you, but I don't smoke."

"Think of it as a token. It goes back to the first time I saw you, at Norman's party."

The lighter had considerable heft, a brushed stainless steel instrument with engraved initials. Turning it in his hand, Charlie tried to make out the Gothic scrawl. "This looks like an M."

"It *is,*" Bianca said with triumph. "M.E."

"I'm sorry?"

"Marlys. Marlys Entwistle."

Charlie shook his head. "This is Marlys's lighter? And you're giving it to me."

Bianca squeezed him affectionately about the chest and shoulders, a gesture that melted Charlie, causing him to grin wider than he'd wished and to feel almost incapacitated with happiness.

"Get dressed," she said. "I have things to show you." She swung her legs over the side of the bed, energized and purposeful. "Quickly," she chided. "We'll have time for more of this after you've seen. It's getting late. Come on, Charlie."

— ❧ —

In spite of some inspired driving from Charlie and expert guidance through the labyrinthine streets of the lower Riviera from Bianca, by the time they arrived at Bianca's destination, the downtown Paseo Nuevo shopping mall, the only establishments still open were restaurants, coffee houses, and a record store.

178

Bianca pouted all the way through the decaf cappuccinos Charlie bought them in an attempt to console her disappointment.

"Do you have a CD player?" Bianca asked at one point, but when Charlie said yes, she shook her head. "What's the challenge in *that*?" she said as if to herself, directed them back to her apartment, where they made love with some abandon until Bianca, mindful of an eight o'clock class to give the next morning, sent Charlie home, bewildered but too happy to complain.

He drove to Bianca's apartment from his final class the next afternoon. Wearing a summer dress with a bright floral pattern and a floppy-brimmed straw hat, she exuded the same kinetic energy of the earlier part of the previous night. Her long auburn hair, held in minimal check by a pair of tortoise-shell combs, emphasized her willowy appearance. In her choice of high-heeled sandals, she made no attempt to compensate for her greater height, rather seeming to emphasize it as she linked her arm through Charlie's to lead them to his car.

All of this, her excitement, her obvious pleasure to see him, overcame Charlie. He sensed in her a purpose that involved him—that involved them. With great abandon, Charlie moved along with her, reminded of times when, as owner of a VW Beetle, he'd been drawn along by the slipstream of a passing semi rig.

"Where to begin?" she said, taking her bearings of the Paseo Nuevo mall, looking about her with great deliberation before looping her arm through Charlie's, giving him a brief nuzzle, then leading them toward Nordstrom's department store.

Charlie was drawn along by a combination of her purpose, her musk, and the exciting sense of being compatible with someone. Whatever she had in mind, it was clear to him that he was the central focus of it. During the next hour, he allowed himself to be led from one department within the store to another, stopping while Bianca examined items of clothing and jewelry for men and for women, cosmetics, cooking utensils, even lingerie, over which she deliberated with an intensity that caused Charlie to redden as he considered the implications. Struggling sometimes to keep pace with her long-legged gait, other times of her

179

hand reaching for his, Charlie found himself responding to the contact of her large cobalt eyes, seeming to ask his approval or evaluation of a particular item.

So much was happening; their exchanged glances were lovers' codes. Charlie was elated. They were beginning to bond, to establish a community of tastes and of mutual dislikes. After more than an hour of this, Bianca led them to the outdoor cafe where the night before they'd had decaf coffee. This time they splurged on hot, frothy lattes. "Now," Bianca said, "let's see how this fits. Close your eyes and give me your hand."

Charlie complied, feeling something of metallic substance being placed on his wrist.

"It fits," Bianca enthused. "We can have it engraved. Just initials. Yours on the outside—" And after a pause— "mine on the inside, if you'd like."

Charlie opened his eyes to see a handsome silver identification bracelet on his wrist. "You're a magician. I didn't see you buy this." He turned his arm, feeling the silver links slide down his wrist. An ID bracelet was out of the range of his taste. This one, while plain and not glitzy, was still a bit too stylish for him. While he was beginning to override these considerations, even think he could get used to such a thing, a greater reality seized him. "This has to be pricey."

"You're pleased, I can tell." Bianca rummaged in her purse. "I know you'll like *this*," she said, drawing out a flat cardboard envelope with the distinctive Yves Saint Laurent logo. Inside the envelope was a pair of black silk women's hose, rich with a tangle of embroidery. "You blushed when I showed you these on the mannequin, and I knew I had to have them."

In the next several moments, Bianca showed him a hair brush with genuine boar bristles, a lipstick with the sheen and color of the skin of an eggplant, a small bottle of bay rum, and a sterling silver pepper mill.

"This is unreal," Charlie said. "I must be blind with love. I didn't see you buy any of this."

Bianca reached for his hand to give him a tug of affection. "Darling Charlie," she said.

"You'll be forever paying for this."

"My dearest Charlie." Her eyes glowed, her hands were warm, and he could feel the pulse in her wrist. "It troubles me that you only have a Timex for a watch." She finished her coffee with a long swallow, daubing a napkin to her lips as she stood. "Macy's has Swiss Army watches," she said, starting purposefully across the cobblestoned mall.

"Am I reading this right?" Charlie called after her. "Is this what I think it is?" He stood, clambering into the table, dancing away from it and in pursuit of her. Was it possible? Had he misread Bianca's expression when he'd first noticed her? Had he interpreted as cool poise and enlightened cynicism what had really been excitement and satisfaction over the successful pinching of Marlys's cigarette lighter? "Bianca," he called after her. "Tell me I'm wrong about this."

Just before she entered Macy's, Bianca smiled back at him over her shoulder. "My blue card, Charlie. Why do you think I'm in therapy?" She blew a kiss in his direction, then plunged ahead.

Getting stuck holding the door for a harried mother with two children and an infant stroller, Charlie said ouch involuntarily when the stroller grazed the toe of one of his Rockports, had to spend the better part of a minute assuring the woman he was not hurt, refuse her paying for a shoe shine. He side-stepped the beleaguered woman, darted into the foyer of Macy's. Then he began to search for Bianca.

With Bianca's height and dramatic appearance, she could readily be spotted among the shoppers—if she were anywhere to be seen. His heart pounding, his blood feeling as though an antacid fizz had been plopped into it, Charlie confronted the thought of leaving right then. Just turn and leave. Dump the booty, the ID bracelet and the bay rum into a trash container. Walk away from Bianca's excitement, the patrician flare of her exquisite nostrils. Flat-out walk away from the memory of her shaking his shoulders to get his attention as she told him she was, for God's sake, drawn to him. Don't forget, this very Charlie Citron whose powers of exegesis may have attracted the editors of refereed journals was still the Charlie who had bored the living hell out of a number of women.

In the same moment he spotted Bianca, moving toward the door where she'd entered the department store, Charlie's newly-acquired peripheral vision from his group mates caused him to see the uniformed rent-a-cop scooting after her, a tall man, as trim as a professional athlete, moving with a purpose of his own.

The Charlie Citron who had much earlier in the game lost a critical beat to Norman Brandenberg in the matter of begging out of this year's reception and the dreary bulk sherry from Solvang was now transfixed in a similar manner. Bianca saw him. She beamed a smile and waved at him. The security guard called after her with some urgency in his voice.

Charlie paused for a moment, swallowed before he started toward Bianca. When he met her, the guard called once again, loud enough to get Bianca's attention. "Excuse me," the guard said, drawing abreast of her. "I couldn't let you get away like this."

Bianca's face shone the way it had, illuminated in the darkness, when she'd lit Marlys's cigarette lighter. "Yes, officer," she said. "What can I do for you?"

Charlie was transfixed by her presence of mind, attracted to her beyond his ability to measure, by all accounts an accomplice now.

"I couldn't let you leave," the security guard said, "without finding out where you got those magnificent combs. My wife has hair like yours. Darker, of course, but every bit as dramatic." He smiled. "Combs like those, do you know what standing a gift like that would put me in?" Bianca put a hand on the guard's arm. "Why, yes," she said. "I think I know exactly."

— ❧ —

Outside in the mall, they leaned against the whitewashed facade of the department store, watching one another for a moment in the flow of shoppers and passersby, then erupting in laughter as the consequences of their excitement, an oxygen debt demanding to be repaid, caught up with them.

"Is there anything else of a startling nature I should know about you?" Charlie ventured while recovering his breath.

She settled into him. "Actually there is. Would it surprise you to learn I'm Jewish?"

"But Bianca isn't a—"

"Exactly. I'm one of four daughters. My parents rebelled at the thought of the traditional names. No Leahs, Esthers, Rachels, or Sarahs for them. We were given pre-Raphaelite names instead. And we've all become academics."

Between gulps of breath, Charlie attempted severity. "Listen to me, Bianca. You can't do this anymore. No matter how good you are at it. You'll be caught."

Bianca was equally concerned with regaining her breath. "I know," she said. "I should stop smoking, too, and pay closer attention to a sensible diet." She considered for a moment. "I have been caught before. Look what it got me."

Charlie put his arms around her. He was already beginning to sense a comfort in the way she fit against him. He was, for a moment, one of his fictional heroes, Dick Diver, the promising young psychiatrist from *Tender Is the Night*, romantically clutching to him his patient, Nicole Warren, in a doorway in Vienna during a sudden downpour and knowing that now her problems were his. "So," Charlie said at length. "Tell me. Did you get the watch?"

Acknowledgments

These stories, some in different form, first appeared in the following publications, whose editors I once again thank: *The South Dakota Review* for "The Ability," "The Man Within," and "Molly" ; *The Pinehurst Review* for "Mr. Right," "I've Got Those King City Blues" (which began life as "Eine Kleine Nachtmusik"), "Absent Friends," and "Messages"; *The Pikestaff Forum* for "Witness Protection Program"; *The Eureka Literary Review* for "Death Watches," "Coming to Terms," and "Between the Acts"; and to my pals across the drink, *World Wide Writers*, for the title story, "Love Will Make You Drink and Gamble, Stay Out Late."

You would think stories that made their way into these journals would get a free pass, but I'm happy to acknowledge that Carol Fuchs and Christopher Meeks of White Whisker had notes on each one, and Lori Braun Anaya prompted an ending Carol was after me to produce.

About the Author

Shelly Lowenkopf taught in the University of Southern California's Master of Professional Writing Program for 34 years, has taught at the annual Santa Barbara Writer's Conference since 1980, and has been guest lecturer in many schools and conferences. He is currently Visiting Professor at the College of Creative Studies, University of California, Santa Barbara, with classes in noir fiction, the modern short story, genre fiction, and developing a literary voice. Mr. Lowenkopf has served as editorial director for literary, general trade, mass market, and scholarly book publishers, seeing over 500 books through the editorial and production process. His own short fiction has appeared widely in the literary press.